PENGUIN CRI

Editor: Julia

MAIGRET STONEWALLED

Georges Simenon was born at Liège in Belgium in 1903. At sixteen he began work as a journalist on the *Gazette de Liège*. He has published over 175 books, many of them psychological novels, and others in the Inspector Maigret series, and his work has been admired by almost all the leading French and English critics. His books have been translated into more than twenty-five languages and more than forty of them have been filmed; his psychological novels have had a great influence on the French cinema. He has travelled all over the world, and at one time lived on a cutter making long journeys of exploration round the coasts of northern Europe. He is married and has four children. His recreations are riding, fishing, and golf.

GEORGES SIMENON

MAIGRET STONEWALLED

*

TRANSLATED BY
MARGARET MARSHALL

PENGUIN BOOKS

Penguin Books Ltd, Harmondsworth, Middlesex, England
Penguin Books Inc., 7110 Ambassador Road, Baltimore, Maryland 21207, U.S.A.
Penguin Books Australia Ltd, Ringwood, Victoria, Australia
Penguin Books Canada Ltd, 41 Steelcase Road West, Markham, Ontario, Canada
Penguin Books (N.Z.) Ltd, 182–190 Wairau Road, Auckland 10, New Zealand

—

Monsieur Gallet décédé first published 1931
This translation first published in Penguin Books 1963
Reprinted 1964, 1970, 1972, 1974, 1976

—

—

Made and printed in Great Britain
by Cox & Wyman Ltd,
London, Reading and Fakenham
Set in Monotype Garamond

CHAPTER 1

Just Another Job

It was on 27 June 1930 that Chief Inspector Maigret had his first encounter with the dead man, who was destined to be a most intimate and disturbing feature of his life for weeks on end. There were several aspects to this encounter, some commonplace, some harrowing, some unforgettable.

The unforgettable aspect was that for a week now the Criminal Police had been receiving a stream of notes announcing that the King of Spain would arrive in Paris on the twenty-seventh, and calling attention to the precautions laid down for such an event.

On top of that, the Head of the Criminal Police was in Prague for a technical Police Conference. The Deputy Head had been called away to his villa on the Normandy coast as one of his children was ill.

Maigret was the Chief Inspector and had to attend to everything. The heat was suffocating, and the staff cut to a minimum for the holiday season.

What is more it was at dawn on 27 June that a woman – a dressmaker – was found murdered in the rue de Picpus.

To cap it all, by nine o'clock in the morning all available inspectors had left for the Bois de Boulogne station, where the Spanish sovereign was due to arrive.

Maigret had had doors and windows opened; the draught made the doors bang and the papers fly off the tables.

At a few minutes past nine a telegram arrived from Nevers:

Émile Gallet, commercial traveller, domiciled Saint-Fargeau, Seine-et-Marne, murdered night of 25th–26th Hôtel de la Loire, Sancerre. Several peculiar circumstances. Warn family identify corpse. If possible send Chief Inspector from Paris.

Maigret had no option but to go to Saint-Fargeau himself.

It was only twenty-odd miles from Paris – an hour before he hadn't even known it existed.

He didn't know the train times. On arrival at the Gare de Lyon he was told the local train was leaving any minute; by dint of running down the platform he was just in time to jump into the last carriage.

He was now sweating profusely. He spent the rest of the journey recovering his breath and mopping himself, for he carried a certain amount of weight.

He was the only passenger to get off at Saint-Fargeau, and he had to wander up and down the soft asphalt of the platform for several minutes before he unearthed a porter.

'Monsieur Gallet? . . . Right at the end of the main avenue in the new development estate. . . . You'll see a notice on the house – it's called Les Marguerites. . . . It's about the only building finished, anyway. . . .'

Maigret took his coat off, slipped a handkerchief under his bowler to protect the back of his neck; the avenue indicated by the porter was about two hundred yards wide and passable only in the middle, where there was absolutely no shade at all.

The sun was a dull copper colour. The flies were buzzing around him unmercifully, indicating the approach of a storm.

Not a soul was in sight to enliven the scene or tell a stranger the way.

The development area was nothing more than a huge wood, which at one time must have been part of a country estate. All that had happened so far was that a geometrical pattern of paths had been cut, as if by a giant lawn-mower, and the electric cables which would one day supply light to the houses had been laid.

Opposite the station, however, there was a square already laid out with fountains and pools in mosaic. A wooden notice-board read ESTATE SALES OFFICE. Alongside was a plan showing that these uninhabited clearings had already been named after generals and politicians.

Every fifty yards Maigret removed the handkerchief and

mopped himself, returning it to the back of his neck, which he could already feel getting sunburnt.

In all directions were buildings in embryo, half finished walls which the bricklayers had abandoned because of the heat.

He had come well over a mile from the station before he came upon Les Marguerites. The house was vaguely English in style, red-tiled and elaborately ornamented with a rough-hewn wall shutting off the garden from what would still be forest for some years to come.

Through the bay-windows on the first floor he saw a bed with a mattress folded in two. The blankets and covers were hanging over the window bar to air.

He rang. A cross-eyed maid of about thirty inspected him first through a judas, and while she was making up her mind whether to open the door or not Maigret put on his coat.

'Madame Gallet, please. . . .'

'Who shall I say? . . .'

But a voice inside was already asking:

'What's happening, Eugénie?'

And Madame Gallet herself appeared at the door, looking down her nose, as if demanding to know what this intrusion meant.

'You've dropped something,' she remarked ungraciously, as he took off his hat, forgetting the handkerchief which fluttered to the ground; there was no welcome in that voice.

He picked up the handkerchief, muttering something unintelligible, and introduced himself:

'Chief Inspector Maigret, No. 1 Flying Squad. I would like a few words with you, Madame. . . .'

'With me?'

Turning to the maid, she said:

'And what are *you* waiting for?'

Maigret knew Madame Gallet's type. She was a woman of about fifty and a definitely unpleasant customer. Although it was still comparatively early and very hot and the house was completely isolated she was wearing a dress of mauve silk, and not a single grey hair was out of place. Her neck, bosom, and hands moreover were covered in a mass of gold chains, brooches, and jingling bangles.

With obvious distaste she led her visitor into the drawing-room. Passing an open door, Maigret had a glimpse of a white-painted kitchen gleaming with copper and aluminium.

'May I start polishing, Madame?'

'Of course. What are you waiting for?'

The maid disappeared into the dining-room next door, and soon she could be heard rubbing wax, as she knelt on the floor; the pungent smell of turpentine spread through the house.

On every article of furniture in the drawing-room there was some kind of embroidery or cover. On the wall hung an enlarged photograph of a tall, thin boy with knock-knees and an unpleasant expression, dressed for his first communion.

On the piano was a smaller photograph of a man with wiry hair and a pepper-and-salt beard, wearing a badly cut morning-coat.

He had a long oval face like the boy's. There was something else odd about it, which Maigret could not place for a moment or two: the mouth was extraordinarily thin-lipped and so wide that it seemed almost to cut the face in two.

'Your husband?'

'Yes, my husband. But all I want to know is what business the police have here....'

During the conversation which followed Maigret's eyes often wandered to the picture; it was in fact his first introduction to the dead man.

*

'I have bad news for you, Madame.... Your husband is away, isn't he?'

'Well! Tell me... Has he?...'

'Yes, an accident has happened.... Not exactly an accident. ... You must be brave....'

She stood straight in front of him, her hand on a small table on which was some cheap bronze ornament. Her face was hard and suspicious; only her plump fingers trembled. What was it that made Maigret think she must have been slim once, perhaps even thin, in early life and that she had put on weight with age?

'Your husband was murdered in Sancerre, on the night of the 25th to 26th. I have the painful task of . . .'

The Chief Inspector turned and pointed to the picture of the boy. 'You have a son?'

Momentarily, Madame Gallet almost seemed to lose the icy calm which she obviously considered essential to her dignity. She said, through tight lips:

'Yes, one son. . . .'

And then, in a voice of triumph:

'You did say Sancerre, didn't you? . . . And today is the 27th. . . . In that case, you are wrong. . . . Wait. . . .'

She went into the dining-room, where Maigret caught sight of the maid on all fours. When she came back she held a post-card out to her visitor.

'This card is from my husband. . . . It is dated the 26th, in other words yesterday, and it is stamped Rouen. . . .'

She could hardly suppress a smile of delight at humiliating the police who had had the effrontery to intrude on her.

'This must be some other Gallet, although I don't know of one. . . .'

For two pins she would have shown him the door; she was looking that way all the time.

'Your husband's Christian name is Émile? And according to his identity papers he is a commercial traveller.'

'He is the Normandy agent for the firm of Niel and Company.'

'I fear, Madame, that you have no cause for jubilation. . . . I must ask you to go with me to Sancerre. . . . For your sake and for mine. . . .'

'But if . . . ?'

She put down the post-card which had a picture of the Old

Market Place at Rouen. The dining-room door was still open; the maid's feet and backside were visible, and from time to time her head and the hair hiding her face too. The polishing rag could be heard swishing across the floor.

'Believe me, I sincerely hope there has been a mistake. But the papers found in the dead man's pocket are definitely your husband's.'

'Someone could have stolen them. . . .'

In spite of herself, there was a note of apprehension in her voice. She followed Maigret's glance to the picture and remarked:

'That photograph was taken when he was already on a diet. . . .'

'If you want to have your lunch,' said the Chief Inspector, 'I will call for you in say an hour's time. . . .'

'Certainly not. . . . If you think that . . . that I must . . . Eugénie! . . . My black silk coat, my handbag, and my gloves. . . .'

*

Maigret felt no interest in this case, which gave every indication of being a thoroughly unpleasant one. And though he already had a picture in his mind of the man with the goatee beard – who was on a diet – and the boy in his first communion suit, he hardly realized it.

All he had to do seemed to be just tiresome drudgery. First the walk back down the famous central avenue, heat even more stifling than before and unable this time to take off his coat; then a wait of thirty-five minutes on the station seat at Melun, where he bought a packet of sandwiches, some fruit, and a bottle of Bordeaux.

By three o'clock in the afternoon he was sitting opposite Madame Gallet in a first-class compartment, rolling down the main Moulins line which goes through Sancerre.

The blinds were drawn, and the windows down, but only occasionally was there a breath of fresh air.

Maigret took his pipe out of his pocket, looked hard at his companion, and finally abandoned the idea of smoking in her presence.

The train had been going a good hour before she asked in a somewhat more human tone of voice:

'How can you explain it?'

'At the moment I am unable to explain anything, Madame. I know nothing. As I told you the crime took place on the night of the 25th to 26th at the Hôtel de la Loire.

'This is holiday time.... Anyway the magistrates in the provinces are never in much of a hurry.... The Criminal Police were informed only this morning.... Did your husband usually send you post-cards?'

'Always, when he was away.'

'Did he travel a great deal?'

'For about three weeks every month. He used to go to Rouen, where he stayed at the Hôtel de la Poste.... He's done that for twenty years, now!... From there he would operate all over Normandy, but he always tried to return to Rouen for the night.'

'You have only one son?'

'Yes, just one. He works in a bank in Paris....'

'Doesn't he live with you here in Saint-Fargeau?'

'It's too far for him to commute every day. He spends Sundays with us....'

'May I suggest that you have something to eat?'

'No, thank you!' she exclaimed, as if the suggestion was an impertinence.

When he came to think of it he could not see her munching a sandwich like any Tom, Dick, or Harry, or drinking tepid wine from one of the railway's greaseproof paper cups.

It was evident that for her dignity was no empty word. She could never have been pretty, but she had good features and, had she been less aloof, she would not have been without some charm, thanks to a certain expression of melancholy in her face, emphasized by the way she held her head, slightly on one side.

'Why should anyone want to kill my husband?'

'Do you know if he had any enemies?'

'No enemies, nor friends! We live a rather lonely life, like all who have known better days do in this post-war period with its brutality and vulgarity. . . .'

'Ah, yes.'

The journey seemed endless. Maigret went out several times into the corridor to have a few puffs at his pipe. His collar had become soft with the heat and because he was sweating profusely. He envied Madame Gallet, who appeared not to notice that it was between 90 and 95 degrees in the shade and sat in exactly the same position as when they left, as if she had just taken a bus, her bag on her knees, her hands on her bag, her head ever so slightly turned towards the carriage door.

'How was this . . . this man killed?'

'The telegram didn't say. . . . I believe they found him dead in the morning. . . .'

Madame Gallet shuddered, her lips parted, and for a moment she seemed to be unable to get her breath.

'It can't be my husband. . . . This card is proof, surely? . . . I shouldn't even have come. . . .'

Without knowing why, precisely, Maigret regretted not having taken the photograph on the piano, because he was now finding it difficult to reconstruct in his mind the upper part of the face. On the other hand he had a clear picture of the very wide mouth, the wiry little beard, and the bad cut of the shoulders of the morning coat.

It was seven o'clock in the evening when the train stopped at the station of Tracy-Sancerre and there was then still over half a mile to do on the main road and then over the suspension bridge above the Loire.

There was none of the magnificent grandeur of a great river here, only a scene of myriads of little streams running between banks of sand the colour of over-ripe corn.

On one of these little islets there was a man dressed in a nankeen suit fishing. The Hôtel de la Loire appeared, its yellow façade running along the embankment.

The rays of the sun were getting lower and lower, but the air, heavy with damp, was still almost unbreathable.

Now it was Madame Gallet who led the way, and Maigret, seeing a man – obviously a fellow-policeman – walking up and down near the hotel, frowned to himself, thinking what a ridiculous couple he and this woman must look.

People on holiday, mostly families, in bright-coloured clothes, were sitting down to dinner under a glass veranda, while waitresses, in white cap and apron, were bustling around.

Madame Gallet had already seen the hotel sign, surrounded by badges of various clubs. She made a bee-line for the door.

'Criminal Police?' asked the man on duty, stopping Maigret.

'Well?'

'They've taken him to the Town Hall. You'd better hurry, because they're doing the autopsy at eight o'clock. You've just got time.'

*

Time to get acquainted with the dead man! Maigret was still trailing along like a man who has a difficult and unpleasant duty to perform.

He had plenty of time later to go over this second encounter in his mind; there could never be another one.

The village looked dead white in the storm-laden afternoon light. Chickens and geese crossed the road and about five hundred yards further on, where there was a patch of shade, two men in blue aprons were shoeing a horse.

Opposite the town hall people were sitting at tables on the terrace of a café; from the shade of the red and yellow striped awnings emerged an atmosphere of cool beer, ice floating in strong-smelling apéritifs, and the Paris newspapers just arrived.

Three cars were parked in the middle of the square. A nurse

was looking for the chemist's shop. In the town hall itself a woman was swilling the grey flag-stoned passage with water.

'Excuse me! . . . The body? . . .'

'Back behind! . . . In the school gymnasium. . . . The gentlemen are there. . . . You can go this way. . . .'

She pointed to a door with GIRLS written above it; BOYS figured similarly on the other wing of the building.

Madame Gallet moved on with unexpected self-assurance. Maigret guessed that it was agitation of mind which was driving her on.

In the school yard a doctor in a white overall was pacing up and down smoking a cigarette, as though waiting for something. Every now and then he rubbed his sensitive-looking hands together.

Two other men were talking together in low voices near a table, on which, under a white sheet, lay the body of a dead man.

The Chief Inspector tried to put the brake on his companion's headlong speed, but he had no time to intervene. She was already in the gymnasium; she stopped for a moment in front of the table, and then with a sharp intake of breath, she suddenly lifted the sheet head high.

She gave no cry. The two men chatting together turned round in astonishment at her. The doctor was putting on rubber gloves, and shouting towards a door:

'Hasn't Mademoiselle Angèle come back yet?'

While he was taking off one of his gloves again, to light a fresh cigarette, Madame Gallet stood without moving, quite stiff; and Maigret kept near in case she should need help.

Suddenly she turned to him, bitterness written all over her face, and shouted:

'How can this be? . . . Who could have dared? . . .'

'Come away, Madame. . . . It *is* him, isn't it? . . .'

Her eyes were darting about: she looked at the two men, the doctor in white, the nurse just arriving swinging her hips.

'What's going to happen now?' she asked hoarsely.

While the embarrassed Maigret fumbled for a reply, she threw herself on her husband's body, flinging a look of anger and defiance round the yard, on everyone present, screaming:

'I won't have it! I won't have it.'

She had to be forcibly removed and put in the charge of the concierge, who left her water buckets. When Maigret got back to the gymnasium, the doctor had a scalpel in his hand and a mask over his face, and the nurse was handing him an opaque glass bottle.

The Inspector unintentionally trod upon a little black silk hat with a mauve bow and artificial diamond clasp.

*

He did not attend the autopsy. Twilight was approaching and the doctor had announced:

'I've seven people coming to dinner in Nevers. . . .'

The other two men present were the examining magistrate and his clerk of court. After shaking the inspector's hand the magistrate said no more than:

'You'll be seeing the local police; they have begun their investigations! It's a frightfully complicated case.'

The sheet was pulled down and there was the naked body.

This ghoulish meeting lasted only a few seconds. The body was just what one would have expected from the photograph: long, bony, and with the hollow chest of the office worker, sallow skin making the hair look very dark, though that on the chest was reddish.

Only half the face was there; the left cheek had been torn away by a bullet.

The eyes were open. It was difficult to say whether his mousey-grey pupils were duller than in the picture.

'He was on a diet . . .' Madame Gallet had said.

And there, under the left breast, a clear, distinct scar in the shape of a knife-blade.

The doctor, behind Maigret, was dancing up and down with impatience.

'Do I have to send the report to you? What address?'

'Hôtel de la Loire . . .'

The magistrate and his clerk looked the other way and said nothing. Maigret, looking for a way out, took the wrong door and found himself floundering about amongst the benches in one of the class-rooms.

It was pleasantly cool in there, and the Inspector stayed a moment looking at some coloured lithographs – 'Harvest Scene', 'A Farm in Winter', and 'Market Day in Town'.

On a shelf were all the standard weights and measures in wood, tin, and iron, ranged according to size.

The Chief Inspector mopped himself. As he came out, he met the Nevers Police Inspector, who had been looking for him.

'Good! You got here! I can go back to my wife in Grenoble now. . . . Would you believe it? . . . I was just off for my holiday yesterday morning when they telephoned. . . .'

'Have you found anything?'

'Nothing at all! . . . You'll see it's quite incredible, the whole thing. . . . If you like, we can have dinner together, and I'll give you some of the details, if you can call them that. . . . Nothing stolen! . . . Nobody saw, nobody heard, anything! . . You'll be jolly clever if you can say why the poor chap was killed. . . . There's just one point, but it probably doesn't mean much. . . . When he stayed at the Hôtel de la Loire, which happened fairly frequently, it was under the name of Monsieur Clément, gentleman, Orléans. . . .'

'Let's go and have a drink!' said Maigret.

He was thinking of the tempting sight of the little café terrace, which shortly before had looked to him like a haven of refuge.

But the appearance of a frothing half-pint did not bring the peace of mind he expected.

'It's the most disappointing case you could possibly imagine,' sighed his companion. 'You'll be amazed! Nothing ties up! And nothing out of the ordinary, either, except that the man was murdered. . . .'

For several minutes he carried on in this vein, without realizing that the Chief Inspector was hardly listening.

There are certain people whose physiognomy you cannot forget, though you may have seen them only once in the street. Maigret had seen only a photograph, half a face, and the pale corpse of Émile Gallet.

And yet it was the photograph which remained uppermost in his mind.

In fact, he was now trying to bring it to life, to picture Monsieur Gallet chatting to his wife in the dining-room at Saint-Fargeau, or leaving the house to catch his train at the station.

Little by little, the upper part of the face became clearer. Maigret thought he remembered that there were dark rings under the eyes.

'I bet it's liver trouble,' he said all of a sudden, under his breath.

'At any rate, he didn't die of liver trouble!' retorted the Inspector from Nevers, annoyed. 'A liver complaint doesn't remove half your face or stab you through the heart!'

Lights from a travelling shooting-gallery blazed up in the middle of the square, where they were dismantling the wooden horses of a merry-go-round.

CHAPTER 2

A Young Man in Spectacles

THERE were now only two or three groups lingering at their tables. Children could be heard on the floor above protesting at being forced to go to bed.

Through an open window came a woman's voice: 'Did you see the big fat man, eh? He's a policeman! And if you're not good, he'll put you in prison. . . .'

All the time he was eating and gazing idly at the scene, Maigret was aware of a persistent droning noise. This was Inspector Grenier of Nevers, who was just talking for the sake of hearing his own voice.

'Ah! If only they had stolen something from him! Everything would be so simple then. It's Monday today, isn't it? . . . The crime took place between Saturday evening and Sunday morning. . . . The fair was on. . . . At a time like that, apart from show-people whom I distrust on principle anyway, there are all sorts of weird folk hanging around. . . . You don't know these country parts, Chief Inspector! . . . Maybe there are even worse characters here than in your Paris slums. . . .'

'In fact,' interrupted Maigret, 'if there hadn't been a fair, the crime would have been discovered immediately.'

'What d'you mean?'

'Just that; thanks to the shooting-gallery and general row, no one heard the shot. . . . Didn't you tell me that Gallet didn't die from his head-wound?'

'So the doctor says. The post-mortem confirms the theory. The man first of all got a bullet in the head. But it seems he could have lived another two or three hours. Immediately after that, he was knifed in the heart, and death was instantaneous. . . . The knife's been found.'

'And the revolver?'

'We searched, but never found it.'

'Was the knife in the room?'

'A few inches from the body. . . . And there were bruises on Gallet's left wrist. . . . It looks as if he seized up the weapon when he was wounded and rushed at his attacker. . . . But he had lost a lot of strength. . . . The murderer caught hold of his wrist, turned it round, and forced the blade into his chest. . . . That's not just my opinion, the doctor thinks so too.'

'So, but for the fair, Gallet would definitely not be dead!'

Maigret was not trying to parade his deductive ingenuity or to show off to his provincial colleague. An idea had struck him and he was pursuing it, curious to see what might come of it.

If it hadn't been for the general hubbub from the merry-go-rounds, the shooting-gallery, and the fireworks, the shot would have been heard. The hotel people would have hurried to the scene and perhaps intervened before the knifing.

Night had fallen. There was nothing to be seen except some moonlight reflections on the river, and the two street-lamps that stood at each end of the bridge. Inside the café they were playing billiards.

'An odd business!' concluded Inspector Grenier. 'Good Heavens! Is it eleven o'clock already? My train's at eleven thirty-two, and it'll take me quarter of an hour to get to the station. As I was saying, if only there had been something missing. . .'

'When do the fairground people finish for the night?'

'Midnight. That's the law!'

'So the crime was committed before midnight, and therefore everyone in the hotel would not have been in bed.'

Each was following his own line of thought and the conversation went on in fits and starts.

'It's the same with this name Monsieur Clément which he assumes . . . the proprietor must have told you. . . . He used to come fairly frequently. . . . About every six months . . . And it must be a good ten years since he came here first. . . . Always as Monsieur Clément, gentleman, Orléans . . .'

'He didn't have the kind of suitcase commercial travellers usually carry around?'

'I saw nothing like that in his room. . . . But the hotel manager will be able to tell you that. . . . Monsieur Tardivon! . . . Hey! . . . Can you come here a moment, please? . . . This is Chief Inspector Maigret from Paris. . . . He'd like to ask you a question. . . . Did Monsieur Clément usually come with a commercial traveller's suitcase?'

'Full of silver,' added the Chief Inspector.

'No! He always had a travelling bag containing his personal belongings, for he was very careful of his appearance. Wait a moment! I've only once seen him in an ordinary coat. Most of the time he wore a black morning-coat, or dark grey. . . .'

'Thank you!'

And Maigret's thoughts went to the firm Niel and Co. for whom Monsieur Gallet had been general representative in Normandy. This firm specialized in gold and ware suitable for presents: trinkets, period-style goblets, silver-plated forks and spoons, fruit baskets, carving sets, sweet servers . . .

He swallowed the tiny portion of almond cake which a maid had put in front of him and filled his pipe.

'A little glass of something?' inquired Monsieur Tardivon.

'Many thanks . . .'

He went off himself for the bottle and sat down with the two detectives.

'So you, Chief Inspector, are the man in charge of the investigation? What a business, eh! And just when the season's starting! Would you believe that seven of my guests left this morning and have gone to stay at the Commerce! . . . Your good health, gentlemen. . . . All over this Monsieur Clément. . . . I'm so used to calling him that. . . . Anyway, who would have supposed it wasn't his real name? . . .'

The terrace was gradually becoming more and more deserted. A waiter was taking the boxed laurel trees which surrounded the tables and lining them up along the wall. A goods train crossed the river, and the three men mechanically watched its reddish glow until it reached the foot of the hill.

Monsieur Tardivon had begun his career as cook in a big house and he still had a certain solemnity of manner and a slightly condescending way of speaking as he leaned towards his companion.

'What is so extraordinary', he said as he warmed his brandy glass in the palm of his hand, 'is that the crime might not have happened at all except for a complete coincidence. . . .'

'The fair!' Grenier hastened to say, darting a look at the Chief Inspector.

'I don't know what you mean. . . . No! . . . When Monsieur Clément arrived on Saturday morning, I gave him the blue bedroom overlooking Nettle Lane, as we call it. . . . It's that road you see on the left . . . so called, because now it's no longer in use it is overgrown with nettles. . . .'

'Why is it no longer used?' asked Maigret.

'You see that wall just beyond the lane, right? . . . That's the wall of Monsieur de Saint-Hilaire's house. . . . Round here, it's usually known as the "little château", to distinguish it from the great old château of Sancerre, which is up on the hill. . . . From here, you can see the turrets. . . . It has a very beautiful park. . . . Well! In olden times, when the Hôtel de la Loire did not exist, this park extended out to this point, and the main entrance with the wrought-iron gate was at the foot of Nettle Lane. . . . The gate is still there, but it is not used because another entrance was made on the embankment, five hundred yards further on. . . .

'Well, anyway, I had given Monsieur Clément the blue bedroom, with windows overlooking this side. It's quiet. No one passes that way, since the road leads nowhere. . . .

'Well, I don't know why, but that afternoon when he came back, he asked if I had another room with a view on to the backyard. . . .

'I had nothing free. . . . In winter, you can choose, because there are only the regulars, some commercial travellers who make their rounds on fixed dates. . . . But, in summer! . . . Would you believe that most of my visitors come from Paris? . . . There's nothing to touch the air of the Loire. . . .

'Well, I told Monsieur Clément it was impossible and I pointed out to him that his room was really better. . . .

'In the yard, there are chickens and geese. . . . All the time they draw water from the well and, although the chain's been oiled, it just goes on creaking. . . .

'He didn't insist. . . . But suppose I had had a room overlooking the yard . . . He wouldn't be dead! . . .'

'Because? . . .' murmured Maigret.

'Didn't they tell you the shot was fired from a distance of at least six and a half yards? . . . The room is only five and a bit. . . . The murderer was outside. . . . He took advantage of the fact that Nettle Lane was deserted. . . . He wouldn't have been able to get into the yard to do it. . . . Besides, the shot would have been heard. . . . Another glass? My round, of course . . .'

'That makes two!' observed the Chief Inspector.

'Two what?' asked Grenier.

'Two coincidences! First there had to be the fair to deaden the sound of the shot. Then all the rooms overlooking the yard had to be occupied. . . .'

He turned round to Monsieur Tardivon who was finishing filling up the glasses.

'How many visitors have you at the moment?'

'Thirty-four, including children . . .'

'No one's left since the crime?'

'Seven, as I told you. A family from the Paris suburbs, Saint-Denis, I think . . . Some sort of engineer, with his wife, mother-in-law, sister-in-law, and her kids . . . Not very well behaved, incidentally, so I wasn't sorry to see them go to the Commerce . . . Everyone has his own kind of clientele. . . . Ask anyone and they'll tell you we only have respectable people here. . . .'

'What did Monsieur Clément do with his time?'

'It's hard to say. . . . He used to go off on foot. . . . At one time, I thought he had an illegitimate child somewhere nearby. Just a guess, but you can't help trying to think up reasons ... He was a very polite man and he always looked sad. ... I never once saw him eat the *table d'hôte*. ... In winter, you see, we have set dinners. ... He preferred to sit all by himself in a corner. ...'

Maigret had taken from his pocket an ordinary little note-book covered in black oil-cloth. He jotted down in pencil:

1. Telegraph Rouen.
2. Telegraph Niel's.
3. Look at yard.
4. Get information on Saint-Hilaire property.
5. Finger-prints on knife.
6. List of hotel visitors.
7. Engineer's family Hôtel du Commerce.
8. People who left Sancerre Sunday the 26th.
9. Announce reward, by town-crier, to anyone who met Gallet Saturday the 25th.

His colleague from Nevers watched his every movement with a rather forced smile.

'Well? Are you on to something already?'

'Nothing at all! Two telegrams to get off and then I shall go to bed ...'

Only the locals were left in the café, finishing their game of billiards. Maigret went to have a quick look at Nettle Lane which had once been the main drive of a large estate and still had an avenue of handsome oaks.

It was overrun with weeds. At that late hour it was impossible to see anything.

Grenier was getting ready to leave for the station and Maigret came back to say good-bye.

'Good luck! But between you and me, it's a rotten job – nothing sensational, nothing to get hold of. ... Quite honestly, rather you than me ...'

The Chief Inspector was led to a first-floor room where

mosquitoes immediately started to buzz round his head. He was in a bad temper. The job on hand was a dull one, unexciting and very ordinary.

Nevertheless, once in bed, instead of going off to sleep, he began to see pictures of Gallet, sometimes only his cheek, sometimes the lower part of his face.

He kept tossing and turning in the damp sheets. He could hear the river's babble as it lapped against the sandbanks.

Each criminal case has its own special features, which you stumble on sooner or later, and which often hold the key to the mystery.

Perhaps the special feature of this one was that everything was ordinary.

Everything was ordinary at Saint-Fargeau! An ordinary house, ordinarily furnished. The boy's portrait as a first communicant, and the father's, on the piano, in a morning-coat too tight for him.

Everything was ordinary in Sancerre too; a cheap country holiday; a second-class hotel.

Everything underlined the grey nondescript character of the affair.

Representative for Niel and Co.; fake silver, fake grandeur, fake style.

A travelling fair, a shooting-gallery, and fireworks to boot.

And to cap it all Madame Gallet's affected airs, and her hat, with its paste ornament, which had rolled in the dust of the school-yard.

*

It was with relief that Maigret learned in the morning that the widow had left by the first train to Saint-Fargeau and that the coffin containing the remains of Émile Gallet was already on its way to Les Marguerites in a hired lorry.

He was in a hurry to be finished with it all. Everyone had gone, the magistrate, the doctor with his seven people to dinner, and Inspector Grenier.

Thank goodness he was alone and could get on with his own definite job.

First: wait for replies to the telegrams sent yesterday evening.

Next: inspect the room where the crime took place.

Finally: consider all those who *could* have committed the crime, and were therefore suspect.

The reply from Rouen was not long in coming. It came from their police:

Staff questioned in Hôtel de la Poste. Cashier, Irma Strauss, admits to receiving post-cards sent her in an envelope by one Émile Gallet and forwarding them. Got 100 francs a month for the job. Has done this for five years and believes former cashier did same.

Half an hour later, at 10 o'clock, a telegram arrived from Niel:

Émile Gallet ceased working for this firm in 1912.

Now was the time for the town-crier to begin his round. Maigret, having just finished his breakfast, was investigating the backyard of the hotel, which revealed nothing of particular interest, when he was informed that a roadman wished to speak to him.

'I was on the road to Saint-Thibaut,' he explained, 'when I saw this Monsieur Clément, whom I knew as I'd seen him a few times, and remembered him particularly because of his morning-coat. At the same time, a young man came out of the farm drive and they faced one another. I should say I was about a hundred yards from them, but I could tell they were quarrelling all right....'

'Did they part pretty soon?'

'No. They went a little way up the hill. Then the older man came back alone. Only half an hour later I saw the young man again in the square at the Hôtel du Commerce.'

'What was he like?'

'Tall, thin ... long face and glasses....'

'What was he wearing?'

'I couldn't say.... But he seemed to be dressed in grey or black.... Have I earned my fifty francs?'

Maigret handed them over, and set off for the Hôtel du Commerce, where the evening before he had had his apéritif. The young man had lunched there on Saturday, 25 June, but the waiter who had served him was now away on holiday in Pouilly, about twelve miles away.

'Are you sure he didn't stay the night here?'

'He would be on our books....'

'Does no one remember him?'

The cashier recalled that someone had ordered vermicelli without butter, which had to be specially prepared.

'A young man who sat over there, you see the pillar on the left. He looked ill.'

It was beginning to get warm, and moreover Maigret no longer felt bored and indifferent as he had done earlier in the morning.

'Long head? ... Thin lips? ...'

'Yes, a haughty mouth, wide.... He didn't want coffee or any kind of drink.... You know the sort of customer....'

Why did Maigret suddenly get a mental picture of the boy in his first communion dress?

He was forty-five. Half of his life had been spent in many different police departments – vice squad, public order, transport, prostitution, railways, gambling.

That should have been enough to stifle hunches or any belief in intuition.

All the same, for twenty-four hours these two pictures of father and son had haunted him, as well as a rather commonplace remark made by Madame Gallet:

'He was on a diet....'

It was no definite plan which made him set off for the Post Office and ask to be put through to Saint-Fargeau Town Hall.

'Hullo! ... Criminal Police here.... Can you tell me when they are burying Monsieur Gallet?'

'Tomorrow, at eight in the morning....'

'In Saint-Fargeau?'

'Yes, here! ...'

'One more question! Who's speaking?'

'The schoolmaster. . . .'

'Do you know Monsieur Gallet's son?'

'Well, I've seen him a few times. . . . He was here this morning for the documents. . . .'

'What does he look like?'

'What d'you mean?'

'Is he tall – thin?'

'Yes. . . . Rather. . . .'

'Does he wear glasses?'

'Wait a second. . . . I remember! . . . Tortoise-shell rimmed glasses. . . .'

'Do you know if he's ill?'

'How would I know? He's pale, certainly. . . .'

'Thank you. . . .'

Ten minutes later the Chief Inspector was back in the Café du Commerce.

'Madame, could you tell me whether your client on Saturday wore glasses?'

The cashier tried to remember, finally shook her head.

'Yes. . . . No. . . . I can't remember. . . . So many people come and go in summer! . . . I even said to the waiter he had a mouth like a toad. . . .'

*

It was some time before he discovered the roadman again. He was drinking away his fifty francs with his mates in a little bar behind the church.

'You told me that your man wore glasses.'

'The young 'un, yes! Not the old man. . . .'

'What kind of glasses?'

'Very round, I'd say . . . with black rims. . . .'

On getting up that morning, Maigret had been happy to hear that the dead man had gone, and Madame Gallet, the magistrate, the doctor, and the police as well.

He hoped that at last he would be left to tackle a definite

problem and that he would not have to go on conjuring up pictures of the queer face of the old man with the beard.

At three o'clock that afternoon, he took the train for Saint-Fargeau.

To begin with, he had only seen a photograph of Émile Gallet. And afterwards he had seen half his face.

Now he would only find a coffin, closed for ever.

However, as the train began to pull out he had the curious feeling that he was running after the dead man.

At Sancerre, Monsieur Tardivon treated his regular clients to armagnac all round, and confided with an air of disappointment:

'He looked conscientious, this chap.... A man of about our age! And what does he do but go off without even seeing the room! Would you like to see where he died?... Surprising, isn't it?... But that's what the Nevers police did.... When they took away the body, they made an outline of it with chalk on the floor.... Careful.... Don't touch anything, will you?... With this sort of thing, you never know where it might not get you.'

CHAPTER 3

Henri Gallet Answers

MAIGRET, who had spent the night at his home in the Boulevard Richard-Lenoir, arrived at Saint-Fargeau on Wednesday just before eight in the morning. On leaving the station, he suddenly changed his mind and returned to ask the clerk:

'Did Monsieur Gallet travel much by train?'

'Father or son?'

'The father.'

'He went away for three weeks every month. He would get a second-class ticket for Rouen....'

'And the son?'

'Practically every Saturday evening he travels from Paris, on a third-class return, and goes back by the last train on Sunday.... Who'd have thought it!... I can see him now, no longer ago than the first Sunday in June, going off for the start of the fishing season....'

'Father or son?'

'The father, of course!... Just look!... You see that little blue punt between the trees over there?... It's his.... Everyone wanted to buy that punt; he made it himself of solid oak, and he invented I don't know how many gadgets.... It was just the same with his fishing tackle....'

Maigret meticulously added this little touch to the woefully incomplete picture he had of the dead man. He looked at the punt, and at the Seine, and tried to imagine the man with the beard, sitting motionless hour after hour with his rod in his hand.

Then he set off towards Les Marguerites; it did not escape him that a somewhat pretentious hearse, empty, was moving in the same direction.

Not a soul was to be seen near the house, except a man

pushing a wheelbarrow, who stopped on seeing the hearse and waited, obviously wanting to see the funeral procession.

The bell at the gate was covered with a piece of crêpe. The front door was draped in black with the dead man's initials embroidered in silver.

Maigret had not expected such a to-do. In the passage on the left was a tray on which was a single card, with the corner turned down; it came from the mayor of Saint-Fargeau.

The drawing-room where Madame Gallet had received the Chief Inspector had been turned into a mortuary chapel; all the furniture must have been taken away to the dining-room. Black hangings festooned the walls; the coffin stood in the centre, surrounded by tall church candles.

For some reason it all looked rather mysterious and questionable. Perhaps it was because there were no visitors, and there was a feeling that none would in fact come, though the hearse was already at the door.

Just the one mourning card, and cheaply printed at that! All this pathetic display! On each side of the coffin there was a dark figure: Madame Gallet, on the right, in full mourning, a veil covering her face, a rosary of unpolished beads in her hands; Henri Gallet on the left, also in black.

Maigret came in silently, bowed his head, dipped a sprig of box-wood in the holy water, and sprinkled it over the coffin. He sensed both mother and son watching him, but neither spoke.

Then he retreated to a corner, intent upon the noises outside and the young man's expression. Every now and then, the horses stamped on the stones of the avenue. Near the window, the undertakers were talking in low voices. And in the room of the dead, lit only by candles, the son's peculiar features seemed more pronounced, and the fact that everything round him was black brought out the sickly pallor of his complexion.

His hair was neatly parted and brushed down. He had a high prominent forehead. Behind the thick lenses of his tortoise-shell glasses it was difficult to catch his uneasy short-sighted eyes.

Every so often Madame Gallet would dab at her eyes under her veil, with a black handkerchief. But Henri never looked steadily at anything; his eyes darted from one thing to another, always avoiding the Chief Inspector, who heard the undertakers' footsteps with relief.

A moment later the hand-cart carrying the coffin was banging against the passage walls. Madame Gallet gave a little sob, but her son merely put his hand on her shoulder and looked in another direction.

The grand hearse with all its trappings was in sharp contrast to the two lonely walking figures, preceded by a somewhat embarrassed master of ceremonies.

It was still warm. The man with the wheelbarrow crossed himself and went off down a cross track, while the funeral procession moved on down the avenue, looking very small in that great sweep down which a whole army could have marched past. A small group of locals stood about in the square, and Maigret, leaving the religious ceremony to take care of itself, went into the Town Hall. But there was no one there. He had to go and rout the schoolmaster out of his classroom, as he was at the same time assistant to the mayor; so the children were left to their own devices for a moment.

'All I can tell you is what's written in our register. Here it is: *Gallet, Émile-Yves-Pierre, born Nantes 1879, married in Paris, October 1902, to Aurore Préjean. . . . One son, Henri, born Paris 1906 and registered in the Town Hall of the 9th Arrondissement. . . .*'

'Are they unpopular with the locals?'

'Well, they had their own house built in 1910 while the forest was being turned into a housing estate, and they have always kept themselves to themselves. . . . They are very arrogant people. I spent the whole of one Sunday fishing in my little punt, only about ten yards away from Gallet. . . . When I wanted something, he gave it to me, but I couldn't get anything out of him. . . .'

'How well off would you say they were?'

'I don't know exactly, because I don't know what he spent on travelling. . . . But for these parts, they would need at least 2,000 francs a month. . . . If you've seen their house, you can tell they don't want for anything. . . . They get all their provisions sent from Corbeil or Melun. . . . There's one other thing, which . . .'

But Maigret had caught sight through the window of the funeral procession rounding the church and entering the cemetery. He thanked the schoolmaster, and from the road heard the first spadeful falling on to the coffin.

He made sure not to be seen, and made a detour to get back to the house, being careful to reach it a little after the Gallets. The maid opened the door and looked at him hesitatingly.

'Madame cannot . . . ,' she began.

'Tell Monsieur Henri that I want to speak to him.'

The cross-eyed maid left him on the doorstep. A few seconds later the young man was silhouetted in the passage. He came to the door and, looking past Maigret, asked:

'Could you not put off this visit to some other day? My mother is very upset. . . .'

'I must speak to you, today. . . . I am sorry to have to insist. . . .'

Henri turned, indicating that the detective had only to follow him. He seemed undecided as to which door to open and finally opened the one into the dining-room, where all the drawing-room furniture had been stacked so that one could hardly move in the room.

Maigret saw the picture of the first communicant laid flat on the table, but looked in vain for that of Émile Gallet.

Henri did not sit down; he said nothing; he took off his glasses to wipe them, which he did with a bored air, his eyelids fluttering all the time against the glare of the daylight.

'You probably know that I am responsible for finding your father's murderer. . . .'

'Which is why I am surprised to see you here at a time when in common decency you might have left my mother and me in peace.'

Henri put his glasses on again and adjusted a cuff that had slipped too low over his wrist. His hand was covered with the same reddish hairs as Maigret had seen on the dead man's chest at Sancerre.

His bony face, with its prominent features, and gloomy expression rather reminiscent of a horse, showed no sign of emotion. His elbows were on the piano, which was sideways on to the wall, so that its green-cloth back was visible.

'I would like to ask you several questions, not so much about your father, but about the family as a whole.'

Henri said not a word but remained standing exactly where he was, motionless, icy, and grim.

'Would you tell me first of all where you were on Saturday, 25 June, at about four o'clock in the afternoon?'

'Before we go on I have something to ask you. Am I compelled to receive you or to answer your questions at a time like this?'

It was the same colourless voice, giving an impression of boredom, as if each syllable was an effort.

'You are perfectly at liberty to refuse to answer. However, I would point out . . .'

'Where did your inquiries show that I was?'

Maigret did not answer, and, to tell the truth, he was taken aback by this unexpected retort, all the more unexpected as the young man's expression gave no impression that he was playing cunning.

Henri let several seconds pass. The maid could be heard answering a call from the first floor:

'Coming, Madame!'

'Well?'

'As you seem to know already, I was there. . . .'

'At Sancerre?'

Henri made no move.

'And there you had a discussion with your father on the road to the old château. . . .'

Of the two, Maigret was the more nervous, because he had the impression that he was beating the air. His words fell flat, his suspicions struck no chord.

The most baffling thing was Henri Gallet's silence; he made no attempt to explain, he just waited.

'Could you tell me what you were doing in Sancerre?'

'I was going to see my mistress, Éléonore Boursang, who is on holiday and staying at the Germain boarding-house, on the road from Sancerre to Saint-Thibaut.'

Almost imperceptibly he raised his eyebrows, which were thick – like Émile Gallet's.

'You had no knowledge that your father was in Sancerre?'

'If I had known, I would have taken care not to see him.'

Still this minimum of explanation, forcing the Chief Inspector into more and more questions.

'Did your family know of this liaison?'

'My father suspected it. He was opposed to it.'

'What did you talk about?'

'Are you investigating the murderer or the victim?' the young man said slowly.

'I shall know the murderer when I know the victim well. Did your father reproach you?'

'No, indeed! *I* reproached *him* for spying on me.'

'And then?'

'Nothing. He said I had not the respect for him which a son should have. Thank you for reminding me of that *today*.'

With relief, Maigret heard footsteps on the staircase. Madame Gallet appeared, dignified as usual, her neck hung round with a triple row of large unpolished stones.

'What's going on?' she asked looking from one to the other. 'Why didn't you call me, Henri?'

The maid knocked and came in.

'The upholsterers are here, to take away the hangings.'

'Keep an eye on them. . . .'

'I have come to get certain information which I believe essential to the discovery of the criminal!' said Maigret in a voice which was becoming a little too dry. 'This is of course not a very suitable moment, as your son has pointed out. But every hour that passes makes the murderer's arrest more unlikely.'

He looked at Henri, who was still just looking gloomy.

'When you married Émile Gallet, Madame, did you have money of your own?'

She stiffened slightly and with a quiver of pride in her voice announced:

'I am the daughter of Auguste Préjean....'

'Forgive me, but...'

'The late secretary of the last Bourbon prince... editor of the Legitimist paper *Le Soleil*.... My father spent his last penny on keeping this paper going – it was a good cause....'

'There are others of your family still alive?'

'I suppose so. I have not seen them since my marriage.'

'Were you advised against this marriage?'

'What I have just said should have explained the situation to you. All my family are Royalists. All my uncles have held, and some still do hold, important positions. They were against my marrying a commercial traveller....'

'Were you without private means after your father's death?'

'My father died a year after my marriage.... At the time of our wedding, my husband had some thirty thousand francs....'

'And his family?'

'I did not know them. He never mentioned them to me. I only know that he had a difficult time as a child and spent several years in Indo-China....'

The ghost of a sarcastic smile appeared on the son's lips.

'I merely ask you these questions, Madame, because I have just heard, on good authority, that for the last eighteen years your husband was not working for Niel....'

She stared at the Chief Inspector and Henri started protesting violently:

'Monsieur...'

'I have this information from Monsieur Niel himself. . . .'

'Monsieur, perhaps it would be better . . .' began the young man, advancing toward Maigret.

'No, Henri! I want to prove that this is false, that it is a wicked lie. . . . Come with me, Inspector. . . . Yes. This way. . . .'

Looking agitated for the first time, she moved out into the passage, where she tripped over the pile of black drapes which the upholsterers were then rolling up. She led the detective up to the first floor, through a bedroom of polished walnut in which could still be seen, on a coat-stand, Émile Gallet's straw hat and a duck suit, which he must have worn for fishing.

Beyond this room was a smaller one fitted out as a study.

'Look! . . . Here are his samples. . . . And these forks and spoons, look, in that hideous *arts décoratifs* style; they do not go back as far as eighteen years, do they? Here is the order book, which my husband balanced at the end of each month . . . Here are some letters on Niel's headed paper which he received regularly. . . .'

Maigret hardly looked. He was sure that he would have to come back to this room, and he preferred to absorb its atmosphere.

Here again, he tried to place Émile Gallet in this swivel armchair planted in front of the desk, with its chromium inkstand and crystal-ball paperweight.

The main avenue of the building estate could be seen through the window, and the red roof of an unoccupied house.

The letters on Niel's headed paper were typed with a fairly normal type-set:

Dear Sir,

Thank you for your letter of the 15th inst., together with your statement of orders for January. As usual we shall await the end of the month to settle our account, and shall also suggest certain measures concerning the extension of your field of activity.

Yours ever,

(signed) Jean Niel

Maigret slipped a few of these letters into his wallet.

'Now what do you think?' asked Madame Gallet defiantly.

'What's this?'

'Nothing.... He liked to work with his hands.... Over there you can see an old watch he took to pieces. In the outhouse, there's a whole pile of things he made, fishing gadgets amongst others.... He spent eight full days of each month here, and his paper work only took a couple of hours each morning....'

Maigret was opening drawers at random. In one he noticed a voluminous bundle of pink papers, entitled: *Soleil.*

'My father's papers!' explained Madame Gallet. 'I don't know why we kept them. The complete set of the periodical is in this cupboard, down to the last number, which my father sold his bonds to finance....'

'May I take the file away?'

She turned to the door as if to consult her son, but Henri had not followed them.

'What can you get from them? They're a sort of relic.... If you really think so.... But tell me, Inspector, what Monsieur Niel has said is impossible, isn't it?... It's like the post-cards! ... I received another one yesterday!... And it *is* his writing, of that I'm sure!... It is stamped at Rouen, like the other one. ... Read it! *All well. Am returning Thursday....*'

Once more her feelings broke through, but only just.

'I am still almost expecting him!... Tomorrow's Thursday....'

Suddenly she dissolved into tears, but they lasted a very short time.... Two or three involuntary sobs. She put her black-bordered handkerchief to her mouth and said hoarsely:

'Let's get out of here....'

Again they had to go through the ordinary little bedroom, with its good-quality furniture, its mirrored wardrobe, two bedside tables, and the imitation Persian rug.

In the passage on the ground floor Henri was aimlessly watching the upholsterers carrying the hangings to a small lorry. He did not even turn his head as Maigret and his mother came down the polished staircase with its creaking steps.

An atmosphere of disorder reigned in the house. The maid, carrying a bottle of red wine and some glasses, went into the drawing-room, where men in overalls were trundling the piano.

'It won't hurt it!' said a voice, obviously not caring if it did.

And Maigret had a feeling he had never had before, a worrying sensation. It seemed to him that the whole truth was here scattered around him. Everything that he saw was important.

But he would have to see it differently, not through this fog of distortion. But the fog was still there, created by this woman who fought against her emotions, and by Henri, whose long face was clamped as tight as a safe; by these hangings, too, which were now being carted away, everything in fact, and above all by Maigret's own embarrassment at feeling out of place.

He was ashamed of the pink dossier he was carrying away like a thief, the significance of which he would have been at a loss to explain. He would like to have stayed longer upstairs, alone, in the dead man's study, and to have wandered round the outhouse where Émile Gallet used to work on his wonderful fishing gadgets.

For a moment he was undecided. Everybody was in the passage at the same time. It was lunch-time, and it was obvious that the Gallets were waiting for the detective to go.

A smell of fried onions came from the kitchen. The maid was not the slightest bit put out.

They all fell back on watching the upholsterers putting the drawing-room in order again. One of them had uncovered Gallet's picture under a liqueur tray.

'May I take that with me?' put in Maigret, turning to the widow. 'I may need it. . . .'

He felt Henri glaring at him with even greater distaste.

'If you must. . . . I have very few photographs of him. . . .'

'I promise to return it to you. . . .'

He couldn't make up his mind to go. Madame Gallet rushed forward as she saw the workmen carelessly carting along an enormous vase of fake Sèvres.

'Be careful! You'll knock it against the door. . . .'

There was always this same contrast between the pathetic and the grotesque, between drama and pettiness; it weighed Maigret down, in this stricken house where he could picture Émile Gallet, the man he had never known in life, wandering about, silent, heavy-eyed as a result of his bad liver, hollow-chested in his ill-fitting morning-coat.

He slipped the picture into the pink file. He paused.

'Please forgive me once more, Madame. . . . I am going now. . . . I should be glad if your son would come with me a little way. . . .'

Madame Gallet looked at Henri with ill-concealed anxiety. Despite her dignified manner, her refined movements, the triple row of black stones round her neck, she too must have sensed *that there was something*. . . .

But the young man appeared quite unmoved; went over to take his crêpe-ribboned hat off a peg.

They left as if in flight. The file was heavy. It was only in a cardboard folder, and the papers threatened to fall out.

'Would you like a newspaper to wrap it in?' asked Madame Gallet.

Maigret was already outside. The maid, with tablecloth and cutlery, was on her way to the dining-room. Henri was striding in the direction of the station, slow, silent, inscrutable.

When the two men had gone some 300 yards, and while the upholsterers were starting up their engine, the Chief Inspector said:

'I have only two things to ask you: Éléonore Boursang's address in Paris . . . yours, too; and where you work.'

He took a pencil from his pocket and wrote on the pink file cover:

Éléonore Boursang: 27 rue de Turenne. Sovrino's Bank: 117 Boulevard Beaumarchais . . . Henri Gallet : Hôtel Bellevue, 19 rue de la Roquette . . .

'Is that all?' asked the young man.

'Yes. Thank you. . . .'

'In that case, I hope that from now on you will concentrate on the murderer. . . .'

He did not wait to see what effect he had produced, but touched the tip of his hat and started back up the main estate roadway.

The lorry passed Maigret just before he reached the station.

*

The last particle of information gleaned that day was just a stroke of luck. Maigret arrived at the station an hour before the train was due. He was alone in the deserted waiting-room, surrounded by a cloud of flies.

He saw a postman arrive on a bicycle, his neck purple as if he could have apoplexy any minute. He put his sacks down carefully on the table used for luggage.

'Do you take mail to Les Marguerites?' asked the Chief Inspector; the postman had not noticed him.

The man turned round at once.

'What do you mean?'

'Police! I am asking you for some information. Was there much mail for Monsieur Gallet?'

'Not a lot! Letters from the firm where the poor man worked. They came on certain set days. Then, some papers . . .'

'What papers?'

'Local papers . . . Specially from Berry and Cher . . . And some reviews: *La Vie à la Campagne, Chasse et Pêche, La Vie de Château . . .*'

The Chief Inspector noticed that the man avoided his eyes.

'Is there a poste restante in Saint-Fargeau?'

'What are you getting at?'

'Didn't Monsieur Gallet receive other letters?'

The postman suddenly seemed at a loss.

'Well, as you already seem to know, and now that he's dead . . .' he stammered. 'And anyway, I didn't break the rules. . . . He merely asked me not to put certain letters in his own letter-box when he was travelling, but to keep them till he returned. . . .'

'What sort of letters?'

'Oh, there weren't very many. . . . Not more than one every couple of months or more . . . Cheap, blue envelopes . . . The address was typed. . . .'

'Did they have the address of the sender?'

'No, no address. But you couldn't mistake them, because there was always typed on the back: *Sender: M. Jacob*. . . . Did I do anything wrong?'

'Where did these letters come from?'

'From Paris. . . .'

'Do you know which district?'

'I looked. . . . But it changed each time. . . .'

'When did the last one come?'

'Wait a minute. . . . It's the twenty-ninth today, isn't it? . . . Wednesday . . . Then it was on Thursday evening. . . . But it was Friday before I saw Monsieur Gallet, he was going off fishing. . . .'

'And *did* he go fishing?'

'No, he gave me five francs as usual and went home. . . . It gave me quite a turn when I heard that someone had killed him. . . . Do you think the letter? . . .'

'Did he go off that same day?'

'Yes . . . Look out, here's your train from Melun. They've just rung the bell at the level-crossing. . . . Will you have to let all this out?'

Maigret ran on to the platform and was just in time to jump into the only first-class carriage.

CHAPTER 4

Royalist Crook

ARRIVING for the second time at the Hôtel de la Loire, Maigret replied without enthusiasm to Monsieur Tardivon, who greeted him with the air of a fellow-conspirator, took him to his room, and drew his attention to some large buff envelopes addressed to him.

These produced the medical expert's statement and official reports from the gendarmerie and the Nevers police.

The Rouen police too had sent further information on the cashier, Irma Strauss.

'And that's not all,' crowed the manager. 'The sergeant from the gendarmerie came to see you. He wants you to telephone as soon as you arrive. Then there's a woman who came three times, most probably after hearing the town-crier's little announcement. . . .'

'Who is this woman?'

'Old Madame Canut, wife of the gardener opposite . . . Do you remember me speaking about the "little chateau"?'

'Did she say anything?'

'She's not such a fool! When there's a reward in the offing, she's not the type to blab out what she knows, always provided she knows anything. . . .'

Maigret had by this time put the bundle of pink papers and Gallet's photograph on the table.

'Find this woman and get the gendarmerie on the telephone. . . .'

A little later, the sergeant was on the line, to tell him that according to instructions received he had collected all tramps within a radius of twenty-five miles and that he was holding them until further orders.

'Anybody of interest there?'

'They're just tramps!' replied the sergeant smugly.

For a few minutes Maigret was alone in his room facing a mountain of papers. And there would be more of them! He had wired Paris asking for information on Henri Gallet and his mistress. On the off-chance, he had alerted Orléans to find out if a Monsieur Clément lived there.

And he had not had time to examine the room where the crime had taken place, nor the dead man's clothes, which had been left there after the autopsy.

At first, the case had seemed a trifling affair. A man who seems a perfectly decent middle-class type is killed by some unknown person in a hotel bedroom.

But now, all the information that was coming in complicated things instead of simplifying them.

'Shall I have her sent up to you, Chief Inspector?' cried a voice from the yard. 'It's Madame Canut. . . .'

A large worthy-looking body entered. She must have tidied herself up for the occasion. She immediately gave Maigret the typically suspicious look of the countrywoman.

'You have something to tell me, I believe? About Monsieur Clément?'

'About the man who's dead and had his photo in the papers. Is it true you're offering fifty francs reward?'

'If you saw him on Saturday the twenty-fifth of June, yes.'

'And what if I saw him twice?'

'Then I dare say you'll get a hundred! Go on, then. . . .'

'First of all, you've got to promise you'll say nothing to my old man. Not because he's loyal to his boss, but 'coz of the hundred francs. . . . He'll just go and drink it. And, of course, I'd like it better if Monsieur Tiburce didn't know I'd spoken up. . . . The gentleman who was killed was with him, when I saw them, you see. . . . The first time was in the morning round eleven o'clock. . . . They were walking in the park both of them. . . .'

'Are you sure you recognized him?'

'Just as I'd recognize you. . . . There aren't many like *him.*

... They chatted there for an hour, maybe. ... Then, in the afternoon I caught sight of them through the drawing-room window. ... They seemed to be arguing. ...'

'What time was this?'

'Just struck five. ... That's twice I saw 'em, isn't it?'

And her eyes were fixed on the hundred-franc note Maigret was taking out of his wallet; she gave a sign as though regretting not having trailed after Monsieur Clément all day Saturday.

A trifle uncertainly she said: 'I think I saw him a third time. ... Probably it doesn't count though. .... Monsieur Tiburce walked back with him to the gate a few minutes later. ...'

'Indeed, it doesn't count!' cut in Maigret, ushering her toward the door.

He lit a pipe, put on his hat and seeing Monsieur Tardivon in the café, stopped in front of him.

'Has Monsieur de Saint-Hilaire been living in the "little château" a long time?'

'Twenty years.'

'What's he like?'

'Very nice. Plump, jolly fellow. Simple and unaffected. In the summer, when the hotel's full, I hardly set eyes on him; after all he's of another class. ... But he often comes here when the shooting season is on. ...'

'Has he a family?'

'He's a widower. We nearly always call him Monsieur Tiburce; it's not a very common christian name. ... All the vineyards you see on the slope there belong to him. He works there himself, goes off occasionally on a spree to Paris, and then comes back to work again. ... What did Madame Canut tell you?'

'Is he at home now, do you think?'

'There's always a chance. I haven't seen his car go by today. ...'

Maigret went up to the gate and rang; he did not fail to observe that, as the Loire made a sharp bend just past the hotel and as the house was the last on that side, anyone could go in or out at any time without being seen.

Beyond the postern gate the boundary wall continued for another three or four hundred yards and then there was nothing but virgin woodland.

A man with a drooping moustache and a gardener's apron let him in; as he smelled of drink the Chief Inspector concluded that he was very likely Madame Canut's husband.

'Is your master in?'

At the same time Maigret caught sight of a man in shirt sleeves examining a water-sprinkler device. He could tell from the gardener's expression that this was in fact Tiburce de Saint-Hilaire, who now left the sprinkler, turned to his visitor, and waited.

As Canut, to say the least, seemed totally at a loss what to do, he finally came over, picking up his coat which lay on the lawn.

'Do you wish to see me?'

'Chief Inspector Maigret of the Criminal Police. . . . Would you be good enough to spare me a little of your time? . . .'

'About the murder, I suppose,' grumbled the squire, hoisting his chin in the direction of the Hôtel de la Loire. 'What can I do for you? Come this way . . . I won't ask you inside; the sun's been beating on those walls all day. . . . We'll be better off here in the arbour. . . . Baptiste! . . . Some glasses and a bottle of the sparkling! . . . Bottom shelf. . . .'

He was just as the hotel manager had described him: small, chubby, red-faced, stubby untidy hands, dressed in a khaki outfit of the type sold ready-made for hunting and fishing; a product of Saint-Étienne.

'Did you know Monsieur Clément?' asked Maigret sitting down on one of the metal chairs.

'According to the papers, that's not his real name . . . he was called . . . what was it? . . . Grelet? . . . Gellet? . . .'

'It was Gallet! That's not very important. . . . Did you have business with him?'

At that moment Maigret could have sworn that his companion was not entirely at ease. Moreover, Saint-Hilaire found it necessary to lean right out of the arbour, muttering:

'That idiot Baptiste may well bring us a medium-dry! . . . And you would certainly rather have a dry, like me. . . . It's my own wine, made the same way as they do in Champagne. . . . About this Monsieur Clément . . . might as well carry on calling him that – what can I tell you? To say that I was in business with him would be an exaggeration. If I said I had never seen him, that wouldn't be quite true either. . . .'

While he was speaking Maigret was thinking of that other interview, with Henri Gallet. The two men had completely different attitudes of mind. The son of the murdered man did nothing to make himself likeable, and he cared little about the peculiarity of his behaviour. He waited for the questions with an air of suspicion, took his time, and weighed his words.

Tiburce, on the other hand, babbled effusively, smiled, waved his hands about, and was everywhere at once, making himself out to be as good-natured as could be.

But with both, there was the same uneasiness underneath, perhaps the fear of not being able to hide something.

'You know. . . . We property owners, we meet all sorts! And I'm not just speaking about tramps, commercial travellers, itinerant dealers. . . . To go back to this Monsieur Clément. . . . Ah! Here comes the wine! . . . That's all right, Baptiste! . . . You may go. . . . I'll come in a minute to look at the sprayer. . . . Now don't you go and touch it. . . .'

He slowly drew out the cork, taking his time, and filled up the glasses without spilling a drop.

'To cut a long story short, he came here once . . . a long time ago. Possibly you already know that the Saint-Hilaire family is a very old one, and I am, now, the last descendant. . . . Still, it's a miracle I'm not a clerk in some old office in Paris or somewhere. . . . If I hadn't been the heir of a cousin who made a fortune in Asia! . . . Well, I just wanted to say that my name appears in all the gazetteers of titled gentry. . . .

'Forty years ago my father was well known for his royalist leanings. . . .

'As for me, well! . . .'

He smiled, drank his wine, smacking his lips noisily in a far from aristocratic fashion, waited for Maigret to empty his glass before filling it up again.

'Our good Monsieur Clément came to see me; I didn't know him from Adam. He made me read several letters of recommendation from French and foreign royalties; he then gave me to understand that he was in some way an official representative of the royalist movement in France. . . . I let him have his say. . . . And the next thing, of course, was . . . he asked me for two thousand francs in aid of propaganda funds. When I refused, he spoke of some old family, I can't remember which, in distress, and said a subscription was being raised for them. . . . From two thousand francs we had already come down to a hundred. I ended up by giving him fifty!'

'When was this?'

'A few months ago! I can't say exactly. It was during the shooting season . . . There was a shoot almost every day at some château in the neighbourhood. I've heard things about this chap practically everywhere I go, and I am sure he was an expert in this sort of confidence trick. But I wasn't going to make a fuss over fifty francs, was I? Your health! . . . The other day he had the cheek to come again. . . . That's how it is!'

'What day?'

'Uh! . . . The week-end. . . .'

'Yes, Saturday! He actually came twice, if I'm not mistaken. . . .'

'You're a wizard, Chief Inspector! Yes, twice. In the morning I refused to see him. . . . In the afternoon he buttonholed me in the park. . . .'

'Was it money he wanted?'

'Dammit . . . Honestly, I can't remember now. What for! But still it was the same old tale about restoring the monarchy. . . . Come on, drink up, it's not worth leaving any in the bottle! Well, what d'you think? Do you think he committed suicide or not? He must have been at the end of his tether....'

'The shot was fired from a distance of twenty to twenty-five feet and the revolver has not been found....'

'In that case ... of course! ... What do you make of it? ... A passing tramp? ...'

'Difficult to believe! The bedroom windows look on to a lane which doesn't lead anywhere except to your estate....'

'To a disused entrance!' exclaimed Monsieur de Saint-Hilaire. 'The gate into Nettle Lane has not been opened for years now, and I doubt if I could tell you where the key is.... What about another bottle?'

'No, thank you.... I suppose you didn't hear anything?'

'Hear what?'

'The shot, on Saturday evening....'

'Nothing at all! I go to bed early.... I only heard about the crime the next day, through my man....'

'And you didn't think of telling the police about Monsieur Clément's visit?'

'Good heavens! ...'

He tried to laugh to hide his embarrassment.

'I said to myself the poor chap had been punished enough! When you have a name like mine, you don't like to get mixed up in the papers, apart from society news.'

Maigret still had the same vague, unpleasant feeling, as if he had a tune on the brain; a feeling that everything about Émile Gallet's death rang false, that everything jarred, from the dead man himself to his son's voice and to Tiburce de Saint-Hilaire's laugh!

'Your staying with old Tardivon? Did you know that he was once a chef in a château? He's lined his pocket since then. Another small one? Really? ... That idiot of a gardener bust the water-sprayer and when you arrived I was trying to mend it.... You have to try your hand at everything when you live in the country.... If you are going to be here a few days, Chief Inspector, come and chat with me some evening....

What with all those tourists, it must be impossible in the hotel. . . .'

At the gate, he took the hand which Maigret had not offered and grasped it with exaggerated cordiality.

Strolling back along the banks of the Loire, Maigret made a mental note of two facts. First, Tiburce de Saint-Hilaire, who must have known about the town-crier's announcement and consequently of the importance which the police attached to Monsieur Clément's movements throughout Saturday, had nevertheless waited to be questioned, and had only in fact talked when he knew that his questioner already knew what had happened.

Secondly, he had lied at least once. He had stated that on Saturday morning he had refused to see his caller, and that in the afternoon he had been *buttonholed* by him in the park.

Now, it was during the morning that the two men had walked in the park. And in the afternoon they were in conversation in the *drawing-room of the house*.

Therefore, the rest was probably false too, concluded the Chief Inspector.

He arrived opposite Nettle Lane. On one side rose the rough-cast limestone wall enclosing Saint-Hilaire's park, on the other the main block of the Hôtel de la Loire, which had no outside staircase.

The lane was blocked with tall grass, brambles, and dead-nettles; wasps were buzzing about to their hearts' content. On the other hand, the oaks shaded the drive completely, and little more than a hundred yards away it ended at a genuine old gate.

Maigret's natural curiosity led him up to this gate, which according to its owner had not been unlocked for years and its key lost. He had hardly glanced at the lock covered in a thick layer of rust, when he noticed that the rust had recently peeled off in places. Better still! On closer examination he spotted unmistakable scratches, the result of a key being inserted into a rusted-up hole.

'Must photograph that tomorrow!' he decided.

He retraced his steps, head bent, going over his picture of Monsieur Gallet in his mind once more, bringing it up to date as it were.

But instead of the detail filling itself in and becoming clearer, it seemed to escape him. The face of the man in the ill-fitting coat just misted up so that it hardly looked human. This mental portrait was the only real picture of the man which Maigret possessed, and in theory it was good enough, but now it was replaced by fleeting images which should have added up to one and the same man but which refused to get themselves into focus.

Maigret saw once more that half of the face, the thin, hairy chest, in the school gymnasium, with the doctor hopping up and down with impatience behind his back. But he also had a picture of the blue punt built by Émile Gallet at Saint-Fargeau, the wonderful fishing gadgets, Madame Gallet in mauve silk, then in mourning, the quintessence of *petite bourgeoisie*, calm and formal.

The wardrobe with the mirror before which Gallet must have buttoned up his coat . . . and all those headed letters from the firm he no longer belonged to! The monthly statements set out with care, twenty years after he had given up his job as commercial traveller! . . .

Those goblets, the sweet-servers *which he must have bought himself*!

Wait a minute! His samples case had not been found, Maigret noted in passing. 'He must have put it down somewhere. . . .'

He had stopped automatically a few yards from the window through which the murderer had sighted his victim. But he didn't even look at the window. He was quite excited, because at that moment he felt that one stroke would be enough to bring into focus all the angles of his picture of Émile Gallet. But then he saw Henri again, stiff and contemptuous, as he had known him, and then at his first communion, his face all screwed up.

The case, which Inspector Grenier of Nevers had called 'a

tiresome little affair' and which Maigret had started in such a bad temper, was getting visibly more complicated as the dead man became a more and more incredible character.

A dozen times Maigret brushed away a wasp circling round his head with the noise of a miniature aeroplane.

'... Eighteen years!' he muttered under his breath.

Eighteen years of faked letters signed Niel, post-cards forwarded from Rouen, as well as the petty ordinary life at Saint-Fargeau, without comfort, without excitement!

The Chief Inspector understood the mentality of crooks, criminals, and swindlers, and he knew that at the bottom of it one always ended up by finding some devouring passion.

And that was exactly what he was searching for in the bearded face, with its drooping eyelids and enormous mouth.

He invented and improved on fishing tackle, and he took old watches to pieces!

At that Maigret rebelled.

You don't lie for eighteen years over a thing like that. You don't get yourself involved in a double life, with all its complications!

This was not the thing that worried him most. You can put up with a false situation for several months or even several years.

But eighteen years! Gallet had grown old; Madame Gallet had put on weight and an excess of dignity; Henri had grown up, he had been confirmed, got his degree, had come of age. ... he was living in Paris and even had a mistress. ... And Émile Gallet went on sending himself letters from the Niel firm, preparing post-cards in advance addressed to his wife, patiently copying spurious order-lists.

'He was on a diet.'

Again Maigret heard Madame Gallet's voice, and he was so absorbed in his thoughts that his heart beat faster and he let his pipe go out.

'Eighteen years without being caught.' It was incredible. The Chief Inspector, who was in the business, understood it better than most.

If there had been no crime, Gallet would have died peacefully in his bed, having put all his papers in order. And Monsieur Niel would have been bewildered when he received notice of his death! The whole thing was so extraordinary that the picture the Inspector was painting for himself produced an inexplicable sense of mental upheaval, the sort of feeling produced by natural phenomena which run counter to our sense of what is real. So it was just by chance that as he raised his head, Maigret saw a dark stain on the white estate wall, just opposite the bedroom where the crime had taken place.

He went up to it and saw that it was a space between two stones which had recently been enlarged and scratched out by the toe of a shoe. There was a similar mark, but less noticeable, a little higher up.

Someone had climbed up there, helped by an overhanging branch. . . . Just as he was about to reconstruct what had happened, the Chief Inspector turned quickly round, sensing that, improbably, there was someone at the river end of the lane.

He had time only to catch a glimpse of a female figure, tall, well-made, with blonde hair and a hard classic profile like that of a Greek statue. The woman moved as Maigret turned, and this seemed to show that before that she had been watching him.

A name came spontaneously into the Chief Inspector's mind: Éléonore Boursang! Until now he had not tried to imagine Henri Gallet's mistress, and yet suddenly he was practically certain that she it was.

He hurried and came out on to the embankment just as she was disappearing round the corner of the main road.

'Just a moment!' he rapped out at the landlord, who was trying to stop him.

And he ran a few steps, taking care that the fugitive should not be able to see him, in an effort to reduce the distance between them. Not only had she the kind of figure which went with the name Éléonore Boursang; she was exactly the kind of woman Henri Gallet would have chosen.

When he reached the cross-roads, Maigret was disappointed. She had disappeared. In vain did he peer through the half-light of a little grocery store, and then into the forge nearby.

Small matter, however, since he knew where to find her.

CHAPTER 5

The Parsimonious Lovers

THE gendarmerie sergeant must that morning have thought that the duties which fall to a detective had certain attractions.

He had been up since four o'clock, and he had already travelled twenty odd miles on his bicycle, first in the early morning cold then in a hotter and hotter sun before he reached the Hôtel de la Loire for the periodic check on the visitors' register.

It was ten o'clock. Most of the visitors were walking by the water's edge or bathing in the river. Two horse dealers were arguing on the terrace, and the landlord, napkin in hand, was making sure that the tables and the little laurel trees in their boxes were in nice straight lines.

'Aren't you going to say hello to the Chief Inspector?' inquired Monsieur Tardivon.

And lowering his voice he said in a confidential tone:

'He's actually in the room where the crime was committed! He has had a great many papers and also some large-size photographs from Paris.'

So it was that a little later the sergeant knocked on the door and apologized for intruding.

'It was the landlord who put me on to this, Chief Inspector, when he told me that you had got as far as the examination of the scene of the crime. I was attracted, I know you have special methods in Paris, and if I don't disturb you, I should very much like to learn something by watching you....'

He was a simple, honest chap whose round, pink face radiated an unaffected desire to please. He made himself as small as possible, which wasn't easy with his hob-nailed boots and gaiters, and his kepi which he didn't know where to put down.

The window was wide open, the morning sun fell full on

Nettle Lane so that, against the light, the bedroom was almost dark. And Maigret, in his shirt-sleeves, pipe in mouth, collar unbuttoned, tie loose, gave an impression of good humour which may well have surprised the gendarme.

'Sit down here, then. But you know there's nothing interesting to see.'

'You are too modest, Chief Inspector.'

This was so naïve that Maigret turned his head away to hide a smile. He had brought into the bedroom everything which had any connexion with the case. After assuring himself that the table, covered with an Indian cloth of a russet floral pattern, could teach him nothing, he had spread out his files, from the doctor's statement to photographs of the scene of the crime and the body which the Criminal Records office had sent him that very morning.

Finally, yielding to an urge which had more of superstition than of science in it, he had placed Émile Gallet's photograph on the black marble mantelpiece, beside the copper candlestick.

There was a carpet on the floor. The oak boards were varnished, and the first investigators had chalked the outline of the body as they had found it.

From outside amid the greenery came a confused hum, very much alive, made up of the singing of birds, the rustling of leaves, the buzzing of flies, and the cackle of hens far away on the road; the regular blows of the hammer on the anvil in the forge beat time for this orchestra.

From the terrace came an occasional blur of voices and from time to time a car could be heard rumbling over the suspension bridge.

'You've got plenty of paper anyway, I would never have believed . . .'

But the Chief Inspector wasn't listening. Deliberately, with little puffs at his pipe, he spread on the ground, where the corpse's legs had been, a pair of black cloth trousers; they were of such close-woven material that although they had already been worn for ten years or so they could, judging by the shine on them, well have gone on for another ten.

Maigret spread out a cotton shirt and in its proper place a starched shirt-front. But the general effect was not realistic, and when below the trousers legs he placed a pair of elastic-sided shoes the only result was to make the whole thing look ridiculous, and rather pathetic.

It certainly did not look like a corpse! It was so unexpectedly like a caricature that the sergeant glanced at the inspector and gave an embarrassed chuckle.

Maigret was not laughing. Ponderously and determinedly he went to and fro, slowly, conscientiously. He examined the coat, and put it back in the suitcase having proved that there was no hole at the point where the knife had struck. The waistcoat which had been torn above the left pocket took its place over the shirt front.

'That's how he was dressed then,' he said under his breath.

He referred to a photograph from the Criminal Records office, and completed his handiwork by adding a very high celluloid collar and a black satin tie.

'Do you see, sergeant? On Saturday he had supper at eight o'clock. He ate noodles as he was on a diet. Then, as was his habit, he read the newspapers while drinking mineral water. Shortly after ten o'clock, he came into this room and took off his coat, keeping his shoes and collar on for a time.'

Actually Maigret was speaking more to himself than to the policeman, who was listening so intently and who felt it his duty to give his approval to each sentence.

'Where could the knife have been at that time? It's a knife with a safety catch, but a pocket model like many people carry around. Wait....'

He bent back the blade of the knife which was on the table along with the other bits of evidence, and slipped it into the left-hand pocket of the black trousers.

'No! That makes a crease....'

He tried it in the right and seemed satisfied.

'There! He's got his knife in his pocket. He is alive. And between eleven and twelve-thirty, according to the doctor, he dies. The toes of his shoes are covered with chalk and limestone dust. Now, opposite the window, on the wall of Tiburce de Saint-Hilaire's estate, I find marks left by the same kind of shoes. Was it so that he could climb over the wall that he took off his coat? He's not the kind of man to make himself comfortable even at home. We mustn't forget that.'

Maigret was moving about, not finishing his sentences, without a glance at his audience, motionless in a chair.

'In the hearth, where the stove has been taken out for the summer, I find some burnt papers.... Let's go through the movements he must have made: he takes off his jacket, burns the papers, scatters the ash with the base of this candlestick (because there is soot on the copper), climbs the wall opposite, stepping over the window-rail, and then returns by the same route. Then takes the knife from his pocket and opens the blade. It's not much; if only we knew the order in which these things and those movements took place....

'Between eleven o'clock and half past twelve, he is here again. The window is open and he gets a bullet in the head.... No doubt about that! The bullet came before the knife wound. ... And it was fired from outside....

'Now, Gallet grasped his knife. He did not try to get out, so it would seem that the murderer came in, because you can't fight a man with a knife if he's twenty feet away.

'Better still! Gallet has had half his face mangled. The wound bleeds but there's not a drop of blood near the window.

'The stairs show that after he'd been wounded he never moved further than about six feet from where he was.

'*Heavy bruising on the left wrist*, wrote the doctor who carried out the autopsy. Therefore, our man holds his knife in his left hand and someone catches hold of this hand and turns the weapon against him.

'The knife goes into the heart and he falls in a heap. He lets go of the knife, but the murderer does not worry, knowing that *only the victim's finger-prints will be found on it.*

'Gallet's wallet is still in his pocket, nothing is stolen, and yet the Official Records office claims that there are tiny fragments of rubber, particularly on the suitcase, as if someone had handled it with rubber gloves. . . .'

'Queer! Queer!' enthused the gendarme, although he couldn't have repeated a quarter of what he had just heard.

'The strangest thing is that as well as traces of rubber, they have found a little rust. . . .

'Perhaps the revolver was rusty!'

Silently Maigret went and planted himself in front of the window, and, seen like that, half-dressed, white shirt sleeves puffed out, and silhouetted against the rectangle of light, he was huge. A thin column of blue smoke rose above his head.

The sergeant remained obediently in his corner, not even daring to move his legs.

'Are you going to come and see my tramps?' he asked timidly.

'Are they still there? Let them go,' and Maigret returned to the table, fluffing up his hair, fingered the pink file, changed the photos around, and then stared at his companion.

'Have you got a bicycle? Would you mind going to the station and asking what time on Saturday Henri Gallet, a young man of twenty-eight, tall, thin, pale, dressed in a dark suit, wearing tortoise-shell rimmed glasses, took the train to Paris? And by the way, have you ever heard of a Monsieur Jacob?'

'Apart from the Bible . . .' the sergeant ventured.

Émile Gallet's clothes were still on the floor, like the caricature of a corpse. As the policeman was making for the door, there was a knock and Monsieur Tardivon called:

'A visitor for you, Inspector. A lady called Boursang who would like to have a few words with you. . . .'

The sergeant would have liked to stay, but the inspector did not ask him to. After a satisfied look round the room, Maigret said, 'Send her in.'

And he bent over the deflated model, paused, smiled, placed the knife over the heart, and crammed the tobacco down into his pipe with a finger.

*

Éléonore Boursang was wearing a light-coloured dress of a discreet cut, which, far from making her look younger, made her look nearer thirty-five than thirty.

Her stockings were well fitting, her shoes clean, and her fair hair neatly done under a small toque of white straw. She was wearing gloves. Maigret had drawn back into a dark corner, anxious to see how she would behave. Monsieur Tardivon had left her on the threshold of the room where she stood for a moment, seemingly confused by the contrast between the strong light at the window and the semi-darkness of the room.

'Chief Inspector Maigret?' she got out at last, coming forward a step or two and turning towards the figure she could still only just make out. 'I am sorry to disturb you, Monsieur....'

He came out towards her into the light, and when he had shut the door he said 'Do sit down.'

And he waited; his attitude gave her no help; on the contrary he put on a rather ill-humoured air.

'Henri must have spoken to you about me; that's why, since I was in Sancerre, I took the liberty of asking to see you.'

He remained silent; but this did not seem to disconcert her. She spoke deliberately and with a certain dignity in some ways reminiscent of Madame Gallet.

She was a younger Madame Gallet, a little prettier than Henri's mother had been no doubt, but equally typical of that same class of society.

'You must understand my position. After this . . . this terrible thing, I wanted to leave Sancerre, but Henri, in a letter, advised me to stay. . . . I saw you two or three times. I heard from the local people that you had been given the job of tracking down the murderer. So I decided to come and ask you if you had found out anything. My position is delicate seeing that officially I am nothing to Henri or his family.'

This did not seem to be a prepared speech. The sentences seemed to come out effortlessly and she had not hurried over the beginning of her little speech.

Several times her glance rested on the knife lying on the bizarre shape formed by the clothing on the floor, but she had not shuddered.

'Did your lover send you here to pump me?' Maigret suddenly rapped out with calculated brusqueness.

'He hasn't asked me to do anything. He is overwhelmed by the blow that has fallen on him. . . . And one of the worst things is that I wasn't able to be near him at the time of the funeral.'

'Have you known him long?'

She did not seem to notice that the interview was developing into an interrogation. Her voice remained the same. 'Three years. . . . I am thirty. . . . Henry only twenty-five. . . . And I am a widow. . . .'

'Did you originally come from Paris?'

'My father was chief accountant in a spinning factory. When I was twenty I married a textile engineer who was killed by a machine less than a year after our marriage. . . . I was due to get a pension from the firm that employed him, but they claimed the accident was due to my husband's negligence.

'So, as I had to earn a living and did not wish to live in a town where everyone knew me, I went to Paris. I am employed as cashier with a firm in the rue Réaumur.

'I started proceedings against the spinning factory. The case dragged on before all the courts. It was only two years ago that I finally managed to win my case and so feel secure enough to give up my job.'

'Were you a cashier when you met Henri Gallet?'

'Yes. He often came to see my employers, as he was an agent for Sovrino's Bank.'

'Has there ever been any question of marriage between you?'

'At first we spoke of it, but if I had been married before the trial my position in court as regards a pension would have been less favourable.'

'You became Gallet's mistress?'

'I'm not afraid of the word; we are as much united, he and I, as if we had been married before the Mayor. For three years now we have been seeing each other every day. He has all his meals with me....'

'However, he doesn't live with you in the rue de Turenne?'

'Only because of his family. They are people of strict principles, like my parents. Henri preferred to avoid any scenes with his family by concealing our liaison from them. But it has always been agreed that when nothing stands in our way and we have enough to go and live on in the Midi, we shall get married.'

Even at the most indiscreet questions, there was no sign of embarrassment in her behaviour. Once when the Chief Inspector glanced down at her legs, she lowered her dress unaffectedly.

'I am obliged to go into details. So, Henri has meals with you.... Does he help with the expenses?'

'It is very simple. I keep accounts as in all well-run households. And at the end of the month he pays me half the amount spent on food....'

'You spoke of living in the Midi; Henri has managed to put some money aside then?'

'Just as I have. You will have noticed that he isn't strong. The doctors have prescribed fresh air, but one cannot have fresh air when one has to earn a living and can't do manual work. I am very fond of the country too. So we live economically. I have told you that Henri is a bank agent.... The Sovrino Bank is small and specializes in speculation. So he is well placed, and anything we could save, here and there, we used to gamble on the Stock Exchange.'

'Separate accounts?'

'Naturally, you never know what may happen, do you, or what the future holds for us? . . .'

'How much capital have you invested like that?'

'It's difficult to say exactly; the money is in shares and it changes from day to day. Between forty and fifty thousand francs.'

'And Gallet?'

'More. He still doesn't dare to launch me in too risky speculations, like the La Planta mines last August. He must have a hundred thousand francs by now.'

'And where have you decided to stop?'

'Five hundred thousand. . . . We reckon on three more years work.'

Maigret now looked at her with a feeling which verged on admiration. But an unusual admiration, heavily tinged with dislike.

She was thirty years old, he twenty-five! They loved each other or at any rate had decided to live together! And their relationship was regulated, like two partners in a business deal!

She spoke of it unaffectedly and even with a certain pride.

'How long have you been in Sancerre?'

'I arrived on 20 June for a month.'

'Why didn't you stay at the Hôtel de la Loire or the Commerce?'

'They're too expensive for me. I am in the Germain boarding-house on the outskirts of the village, where I pay only twenty-two francs a day. . . .'

'Henri came on the 25th? What time?'

'He is only free on Saturdays and Sundays; on Sunday it was agreed that he would spend the day at Saint-Fargeau. He came by train on Saturday morning. He left by the last train in the evening.'

'Which was?'

'The 11.32. . . . I went with him to the station.'

'Did you know that his father was here?'

'Henri told me that he had met him. He was furious, because he was convinced that his father had only come to spy on us. Henri didn't want his family to interfere in our relationship.'

'Were the Gallets aware of this hundred thousand francs?'

'Certainly. Henri was of age; he had a perfect right to make his own life.'

'How did your lover use to speak of his father?'

'He rather disapproved of his lack of ambition. He would say it was unhealthy at his age still to be selling what he called his "knick-knacks". But he was always very respectful, particularly about his mother.'

'He did not know then that Émile Gallet was really nothing more than a confidence trickster?'

'A crook? Monsieur Gallet?'

'And that for eighteen years he had nothing to do with knick-knacks.'

'It isn't possible!'

Was it an act that she now looked at the grim dummy with a kind of admiration?

'I am stunned, Inspector! Monsieur Gallet! With his strange crazes, ludicrous clothes, looking like a poor pensioner!'

'What were you doing on Saturday afternoon?'

'Henri and I walked on the hill; it was after he left me to go to the Hôtel du Commerce that he met his father. . . . We saw each other again at eight o'clock that evening and wandered around again, this time on the other side of the river, before the train left. . . .'

'Did you pass near this hotel?'

'It was better to avoid a meeting.'

'You came back alone from the station, you crossed the bridge. . . .'

'And turned immediately left to get back to the Germain boarding-house. I don't like going about the streets at night.'

'Do you know Tiburce de Saint-Hilaire?'

'Who is he? I have never heard the name. Inspector, I hope you don't suspect Henri?' She looked agitated, but she kept calm.

'I have come here largely because I know him. He has not been well most of his life, and his character has become gloomy, and suspicious. . . . Sometimes when we are together, hours will go by without a word being spoken.

'It is just a coincidence that he happened to meet his father here, though I know it seems fishy. He is too proud to defend himself. I don't know what he told you. . . . Did he simply reply to your questions? All that I can swear to you is that he did not leave me from eight o'clock that evening until the moment he got into the train. He was nervous. . . . He was afraid his mother would get to know of our relationship, because he always had a great deal of affection for her and he knew she would try to turn him against me.

'I am not a young girl any more, there are five years between us. Besides, I have been his mistress. . . .

'I am, particularly for Henri's sake, anxious to know whether you have got the murderer safely locked up. He is intelligent enough to know that his meeting with his father must necesarily make him uncomfortably suspect.'

Maigret was still looking at her with the same air of surprise. And he was wondering why what she had done failed to move him, when after all it was really very creditable.

Even though her last sentences were spoken with just a shade of vehemence, Éléonore Boursang remained in complete control of herself.

He contrived to uncover a large photograph from the Criminal Records office, representing the body as it had been found, but the young woman merely gave this sensational picture a passing glance.

'Have you discovered anything?'

'Do you know a Monsieur Jacob?'

She looked at him as though inviting him to question her sincerity.

'I don't know that name. Who is he? The murderer?'

'Perhaps,' he let out, moving towards the door.

Éléonore Boursang left as she had come.

'Do you mind if I come to ask you for news from time to time, Inspector?'

'Whenever you like.'

The sergeant was patiently waiting in the corridor. He glanced questioningly at the Chief Inspector after the visitor had disappeared.

'What did they say at the station?' asked Maigret.

'The young man took the train for Paris at eleven-thirty-two with a third-class ticket.'

'And the crime was committed between eleven and twelve-thirty,' murmured the Chief Inspector dreamily. 'If you hurry you can get to Tracy Sancerre from here in ten minutes. The murderer could have done it between eleven and eleven-twenty.... If you need ten minutes to get to the station, you don't need any more to return. So Gallet could have been killed between eleven-forty-five and twelve-thirty *by someone coming from the station....*'

'Only there is the matter of the gate.'

'Yes, there's that! And what the devil was Émile Gallet going to do on the wall?'

The sergeant sat in the same place as before and nodded, waiting for more. But nothing more came.

'Let's go and have a drink,' said Maigret.

CHAPTER 6

A Meeting on the Wall

'STILL nothing?'

'*Obole.*'

'What was that?'

'*Préparatifs*! At least I suppose that's it. The "*tifs*" is missing . . . it could be "*-tion*".'

Maigret sighed, shrugged his shoulders, and left the cool room, where since morning, a tall young man, thin and red-haired, with irregular but pleasant features, and the imperturbability of the northerner, was bent over the table, working at a job which would have discouraged a saint. He was called Joseph Moers, and it was obvious from his accent that he was of Flemish origin.

He worked in the laboratories of the Criminal Records office, and had come to Sancerre at Maigret's request; he was now installed in the dead man's room where he had laid out his instruments, one of which was an odd kind of spirit stove.

Since seven o'clock that morning he had not raised his head except when the Chief Inspector would come in suddenly or lean out of the window overlooking Nettle Lane.

'Nothing?'

'*Je vous. . . .*'

'Eh?'

'I have just found *Je vous. . . .* But still the *s* is missing.'

He had spread out on the table some very thin pieces of glass, which from time to time he smeared with a liquid glue solution heated on the stove. Every so often, he would go to the fireplace, carefully extract one of the pieces of burnt paper, and place it on a sheet of glass. The ashes were fragile, brittle, and crumbled easily. Sometimes it took five minutes to soften them in the steam, after which he would stick them to the glass.

In front of him Joseph Moers had a tool kit which was little less than a portable laboratory. The largest of the pieces of burnt paper were two or three inches across. The smallest were little more than dust.

Obole . . . Prépara . . . Je vous. . . .

This was the result of two hours' work, but, unlike Maigret, Moers was not impatient and did not turn a hair at the thought that he had examined only about one-seventh of the contents of the fire-place.

For some time now a big blue fly, glinting like metal, had been buzzing round his head. Three times it had landed on his frowning forehead, but he had not attempted to brush it away. Perhaps he hadn't even noticed it.

'The trouble is when you come through the door you start a draught,' he said at last to Maigret. 'You have already made me lose one bit of charred paper that way.'

'All right, I'll come through the window. . . .'

This was no joke; he did it. The files were still in this room which Maigret had chosen as his workroom and where even the clothes he had spread on the floor and fixed with the knife had not been disturbed.

Maigret was impatient for the result of this expert examination he had arranged and could not keep still while waiting.

Every quarter of an hour or so he could be seen, head bent, hands behind his back, walking in the sun-drenched lane. Then he would climb over the window-sill, red from the sun and glistening with sweat, he would mop himself, grumbling: 'It's not moving very fast!'

Did Moers hear him or not? His movements continued as delicate as those of a manicurist and he worried only about the sheets of glass which were covered with irregular black stains.

Maigret was particularly impatient because he had nothing to do, or rather, he preferred not to try to prove anything before being certain about the papers burnt on the night of the crime. And while he paced up and down the lane, where through the leaves of the oak trees light and shade danced over him, he went over and over the same line of thought in his mind.

Henri and Éléonore Boursang could have killed Gallet . . . before going to the station. . . . Éléonore could have come back to kill him herself after her lover's departure. . . . Then there was this wall and the key! And in addition a Monsieur Jacob whose letters Gallet had hidden, apparently in fear. . . .

Ten times he went to examine the lock of the gate, but failed to discover anything new. Then, as he was passing the spot where Émile Gallet had climbed the wall, he suddenly came to a decision, removed his coat, and placed the tip of his right foot in the first crack between the stones.

He weighed a good sixteen stone, but all the same he had no difficulty in laying hold of some overhanging branches, and as soon as he had a firm grip of them it was child's play to reach the top.

The wall had been built with rough-hewn quarry stones, covered with a coating of lime. The top consisted of a row of bricks placed edgewise, now covered with moss and quite healthy-looking grass.

'Anything new?' he called to him.

'An *s* and a comma. . . .'

Instead of oak leaves the Inspector found that above his head were branches of an enormous beech growing on the estate.

He knelt down, because the top of the wall was not very wide and he wasn't sure of his balance, examined the moss right and left, and muttered:

'Well! Well! . . .'

The discovery was not sensational; it was simply that the moss had been trodden on and half torn up in one spot immediately above the cracks in the stonework, but nowhere else. Since the moss was easily disturbed, as his experiment had shown, this meant that he could now be quite certain that Émile Gallet had not walked along the wall, that he had not moved a yard in either direction along it.

'It remains to be seen whether he came down on the estate side. . . .'

This area was not strictly speaking part of the park now; most probably because it was hidden by numerous trees, it was used as a rubbish dump. A dozen yards away from Maigret was a collection of large empty barrels, out of shape or without their metal bands. One could see old bottles too, many of them patent medicines, some chests and a long-handled scythe the worse for wear, rusty tools and bundles of old numbers of a magazine tied up with string; sodden with rain, scorched and discoloured by the sun, and stained with earth, they were a sorry sight.

Before coming down from the wall, Maigret made sure that there were no marks on the ground below, in other words below the spot where Gallet had been. So that he should not make marks on the wall, he jumped down and got clear by falling on all fours.

A few glimpses of white through the trees were all that could be seen of Tiburce de Saint-Hilaire's house. An engine was throbbing, and Maigret knew from his investigations that morning that it pumped the water from the well to the tanks in the house.

Because of the rubbish the place was humming with flies. Every few seconds the Chief Inspector had to flick them away, which he did with increasing bad temper.

'The wall first. . . .'

This was easy, for on both sides the boundary wall had been lime-washed in the spring. Now, below the spot where Émile Gallet had climbed, not a mark or a scratch was to be seen. Moreover, within a radius of ten yards there was not a single trace of footprints.

On the other hand, near the papers and bottles, the detective noticed that a barrel had been dragged a distance of two or three yards, and positioned at the foot of the wall. It was still there. He climbed on to it, and his head came over the wall exactly thirty-five feet from the point where Gallet had been.

From where he was, he could see Moers still working, not even stopping to wipe the sweat off himself.

'Nothing?'

'*Clignancourt*; but I think I have a better piece here.'

The moss on the wall above the barrel was not torn, but flattened as if someone had leant his arms on it. Maigret tried it out, leant on his elbows a little farther on, and got an identical result.

'In other words, Émile Gallet climbed on to the wall, but *did not come down on the park side.*

'Someone or other from inside the estate raised himself on this barrel, *but got no higher and did not leave the park, at least not by road. . . .*'

If the people prowling about at night had been some young man and his girl all this might more or less have made sense. Though even then whoever was inside the park could have got nearer his companion by moving the barrel. But this was no lovers' meeting; one of the two was unquestionably Monsieur Gallet, who had taken off his coat on purpose to carry out this operation, which was so out of character for him.

Could the other have been Tiburce de Saint-Hilaire?

The two men had seen each other first in the morning, then in the afternoon, and had made no secret of the fact. It was hardly likely that they had decided to go to these lengths to see each other again, and in the dark!

And thirty-five feet away! If they had been speaking in low voices they would not have been able to hear what the other said!

Unless they came separately, one first, the other later. . . .

But which of them had climbed first on to the wall? And had the two met each other?

From the barrel to Gallet's room the distance was about twenty-two feet, which was the distance from which the shot had been fired.

As Maigret turned round, he saw the gardener looking at him somewhat apprehensively.

'Oh, it's you ...' said the Chief Inspector. 'Is your master here?'

'He's gone fishing.'

'You know I'm from the police – I should like to get out of here another way rather than jumping from this wall. Would you open the gate at the end of Nettle Lane for me?'

'That's easy!' the man said, moving off in that direction.

'Do you have the key?'

'No! You'll see ...'

When he arrived at the gate, he put his hand without hesitation into a crack between two stones, but then gave an exclamation of astonishment.

'Well, I never!'

'What?'

'It's not there any more! ... I put it back myself a year ago when the three oaks were cut down and carted away this way.'

'Did your master know it was here?'

'Of course.'

'Do you remember seeing him come this way?'

'Not since last year ...'

The outline of a new theory was already forming in the Chief Inspector's mind: Tiburce de Saint-Hilaire, on top of the barrel, firing at Gallet, going round by the gate, jumping into his victim's room. But it was so improbable! Even supposing that the rusty lock opened easily, it would have taken three minutes to cover the distance between the two points. And, during those three minutes, Émile Gallet, with half his face gone, had neither shouted, nor fallen, had done nothing but take his knife out of his pocket to meet a possible attacker!

It rang false! It jarred as the gate must have jarred! And yet this was the only hypothesis which followed logically from the evidence of the facts.

At any rate there was a man behind the wall. That was now established fact, but there was nothing to prove that this man was Saint-Hilaire, except the story of the lost key and the fact that the unknown person was in the grounds of the estate.

On the other hand, two other people closely connected with Émile Gallet and possibly having an interest in his death were at Sancerre at that time, and they had no good alibi to prove that they had not been in Nettle Lane: they were Henri Gallet and Éléonore.

Maigret swatted a horse-fly on his cheek and saw Moers leaning out of the window.

'Chief Inspector!'

'Something new?'

But the Fleming had already disappeared back into the room. Before going round by the embankment, Maigret gave the gate a little push, and to his surprise it gave.

'Hullo! It's not closed!' exclaimed the gardener bending over the lock. 'That's queer, isn't it?'

Maigret was about to warn him not to speak to Saint-Hilaire about his visit, but, summing up the man, he reckoned him to be too stupid and preferred not to complicate matters.

'Why did you call me?' he asked Moers a few minutes later.

The latter had lighted a candle and was looking through the glass plate, now almost entirely covered in black.

'Do you know a Monsieur Jacob?' he asked, throwing back his head to look with satisfaction at the general effect of his work.

'Rather! So what?'

'So nothing! One of the burnt letters is signed *Monsieur Jacob*.'

'Is that all?'

'Practically. It is written on ruled paper torn from a note-book or an account book. I have only made out a few words on this kind of paper. *Absolument* . . . at least, that's only what I guess, for the first two letters are missing. *Lundi* . . .'

Maigret waited for more, eyebrows puckered, teeth clamped on the stem of his pipe.

'And?'

'There's the word *prison* underlined twice. . . . Unless a

piece has got lost and it's *prisonnier*, or *prisonnière*. Now I've got *numéra* . . . I can only think of one word beginning like that . . . *numéraire* . . . for it's hardly likely that the letter talks of *numérateur*. Besides, somewhere else there is the number 20,000. . . .'

'No address?'

'I have just told you: *Clignancourt*. Unfortunately, I can't piece the words together in order.'

'The handwriting?'

'There is no handwriting, it's typed.'

Monsieur Tardivon had taken to looking after Maigret himself, and he did this with a great show of discretion as well as the faintest tinge of the familiarity of an accomplice.

'A telegram, Inspector!' he cried before even knocking.

He very much wanted to get into the room where Moers' mysterious work intrigued him. Seeing that the detective was waiting to close the door again, he asked slyly:

'Is there anything I can get you?'

'Nothing at all!' snapped Maigret as he tore the wrapper from the telegram.

It came from the Paris Criminal Police, whom the Chief Inspector had asked to supply certain information. It read:

Émile Gallet leaves no will. Effects consist of Saint-Fargeau house valued 100,000 furnished and 3,500 francs in bank.

Aurore Gallet draws life insurance 300,000 taken out by her husband in 1925, with Abeille Company.

Henri Gallet returned to work Thursday Sovrino's Bank. Éléonore Boursang absent Paris on holiday in Loire.

'Well, I never!' grumbled Maigret, looking fixedly into space for a few seconds and then turning to Joseph Moers.

'Do *you* know anything about insurance?'

'That depends . . .' the young man replied modestly; his pince-nez were so tight that his whole face seemed pinched.

'In 1925 Gallet was over forty-five . . . and had a liver complaint. How much do you think he would have to pay each year to get a life insurance of 300,000 francs?'

Moers made silent calculations, his lips moving; this went on for just under two minutes. Then he said:

'About 20,000 francs a year. It can't have been easy to get a company to accept that risk!'

Maigret darted an angry look at the picture, which was still on the mantelpiece, leaning at the same angle as on the piano at Saint-Fargeau.

'Twenty thousand! And he spent barely two thousand a month. In other words, almost half of what he managed to extract from the supporters of the Bourbons.'

Turning away from the picture he stared at the black shapeless trousers, shiny and baggy at the knees, stretched out on the floor-boards. And he thought back to Madame Gallet in her mauve silk dress, with her jewellery and her acid voice.

One almost expected to hear him say to the picture:

'You loved her as much as that?'

At last, shrugging his shoulders, he turned to the wall baking in the sun, where just eight days before, Émile Gallet had hoisted himself up in his shirt-sleeves, his starched dicky ballooning out of his waistcoat.

'There are still some more ashes!' he said to Moers, and his voice was a little weary. 'See if you can find something else on this Monsieur Jacob. Now, who was that moron who told me he only knew the name Jacob from the Bible?'

A little boy, freckled all over his face, was leaning on the window with a broad grin, while from the terrace a man's voice ordered somewhat feebly:

'Will you let the gentleman get on with his work, Émile!'

'Hullo! Another Émile!' groaned Maigret. 'But at least this one's alive while the other . . .'

But he was sufficiently in control of himself to go out without looking at the picture.

CHAPTER 7

Joseph Moers' Ear

THE weather was still in the dog-days. Every morning the papers were full of reports of storm-damage in various parts of France; for over three weeks now not a drop of rain had fallen on Sancerre. In the afternoon, the room which had been Émile Gallet's was flooded with sun and became unbearably hot.

On this Saturday, however, Moers did no more than lower the rough linen blind over the open window, and less than half an hour after his lunch was again poring over his glass plates and his bits of charred paper, working with the regularity of a metronome.

For several minutes, Maigret hung round him, fingering things, shuffling his feet, like a man who couldn't make up his mind. At last he sighed:

'Listen, old chap! I can't go on like this! I admire you, but you don't weigh sixteen stone. I must go out and get a breath of fresh air.'

Where could shelter be in this heat? On the pavement in front of the café there was a little breeze, but the hotel guests and their children were there too. In the café you couldn't spend half an hour without hearing the irritating click of billiard balls.

Maigret reached the yard, which was half in the shade, and called to a young maid who was passing:

'Would you bring me a deck-chair?'

'Do you really want to sit here? You'll get all the noise from the kitchen.'

He preferred that, and the clucking of hens too, to other people's chatter. He pulled his chair over near the well, spread a newspaper over his face to protect himself from the flies, and it wasn't long before he gave in to a luxurious sensation of drowsiness.

Little by little the din of the plates being washed in the scullery became part of another world, and the all-pervading hold which the dead man seemed to have established over Maigret faded as he dozed.

What precisely was the moment when he caught a sound like two shots from a gun? They did not shake him completely out of his stupor, because immediately a dream built up in his mind to explain away these unsuitable noises.

He was sitting on the terrace outside the hotel. Tiburce de Saint-Hilaire came by in a bottle-green suit, followed by a dozen long-eared dogs . . .

'You were asking me the other day whether there was any game around here?' he said.

He put up his gun, loosed off at random, and down came a host of partridges, like dead leaves.

'Inspector! Quick!'

He sprang up, and saw one of the waitresses in front of him.

'In the bedroom – gun shots.'

The Chief Inspector was ashamed of being so slow to react. People were already running into the hotel, and he was by no means the first to reach Gallet's room, where he saw Moers standing near the table, both hands up to his face.

'Everybody out!' he ordered.

'Shall I call a doctor?' asked Monsieur Tardivon. 'There's blood. . . . Look.'

'Yes. . . . Quick!'

Once the door was closed, he went straight to the young man from the Criminal Records office. He felt guilty. 'What is it, old chap?'

He could see clear enough; and was there blood! Blood everywhere, on Moers' hands, his shoulders, on the glass plates, and on the floor!

'It's not serious, Inspector. My ear. . . . Just here . . .' and for a moment he let go the lobe of his left ear and immediately the blood spurted out. Moers was pale as death. Still he tried to smile, and still more to stop the twitching of his jaw.

The blind was still down, keeping out the sun, so that there was an orange-coloured glow in the room.

'There's no danger in this, is there?' There's nothing like an ear for bleeding. . . .'

'Keep quiet! Try not to pant.' The Fleming could hardly speak, his teeth were chattering so.

'I ought not to get like this. . . . But I'm not used to it! I was just getting up to get some new plates. . . .'

He dabbed at his ear with his handkerchief, red with blood, leaning on the table with his other hand.

'You see! I was right here . . . I heard a shot . . . I swear to you I felt the blast of a bullet; it passed so close to my eyes that I thought my pince-nez had gone. I staggered back . . . and at that moment there was another shot. I thought I was dead! There was a noise in my head, as if my brain were on fire. . . .'

He smiled more naturally. 'You see it's nothing! A little bit of my ear off . . . I should have run to the window. . . . But I couldn't move. . . . I thought there might be more bullets to come. . . . I didn't know what a bullet was like before. . . .'

He had to sit down. His legs began to give way under him; it was a sort of delayed action shock, fear in retrospect.

'Don't worry about me. . . . Find the . . .'

Drops of sweat glistened on his forehead and Maigret, realizing that he was going to faint, ran to the door.

'Where's the manager? You look after him. . . . Where's the doctor?'

'He's not at home. But one of my guests is a nurse at the Hôtel Dieu . . .'

Maigret drew back the blind and swung his legs over the window-sill, mechanically stuffing his unlit pipe into his mouth. Nettle Lane was deserted, half in the shade and the other half shimmering with heat and light. At the end, the Louis XIV gate was shut.

The Chief Inspector noticed nothing unusual on the white

wall opposite the room. As for footprints, it was no good looking for them here in the parched grass; that carried no prints any more than does bare stony earth.

He walked towards the embankment. A score of people had gathered there, undecided whether to come nearer or not.

'Which of you were on the terrace when the shots were fired?'

Several voices replied: 'I was!' Excited and eager, they stepped forward.

'Did you see anyone go into this lane?'

'Not a soul! Not for an hour anyway. I myself haven't moved from this spot!' said a wizened little man in a multicoloured sweater. 'Go back to your mother, Charlie! . . . I was here, Inspector. If the murderer had gone up Nettle Lane I'd have seen him, definitely. . . .'

'Did you hear the shots?'

'Everyone did. I imagined they were shooting on the estate next door. . . . I even went a step or two up . . .'

'And you didn't see anyone in the lane?'

'Nobody at all. . .'

'You didn't look behind every tree, of course!' Maigret said so quickly to set his conscience at rest, and then set off for the main entrance of the 'little château'. The gardener was pushing a wheelbarrow full of gravel down a path.

'Isn't he here?'

'He's probably at the notary's. They usually play cards at this time of day.'

'Did you see him leave?'

'Indeed I did! More than an hour and a half ago that was.'

'And you've seen no one in the park?'

'Nobody. . . . Why?'

'Where were you ten minutes ago?'

'By the river bank, loading the gravel.'

Maigret looked him in the eye; the man seemed honest, besides, he was too stupid to be a good liar.

Without worrying about him further, the Chief Inspector went up to the barrel against the wall of the enclosure, but there were no signs here that a murderer had been around.

He examined the rusty gate with no better luck. It did not seem to have been opened since the morning, when he himself had pushed through it.

'Nevertheless, two shots were fired!'

In the hotel the guests had finally sat down again, but everyone was talking now.

'It's not serious,' said Monsieur Tardivon, coming to meet the Chief Inspector. 'I have just heard that the doctor is at Petit's, the notary's house. . . . Shall I send someone for him?'

'Where is the notary's house?'

'In the square, next door to the Café du Commerce . . .'

'Whom does this bicycle belong to?'

'I don't know. You can take it. . . . Are you going there yourself?'

Maigret mounted the bicycle, which was too small for him; the saddle springs creaked. Five minutes later he was pulling at the bell of a vast house, clean and cool-looking; an old maid in a blue gingham apron looked at him through the judas.

'Is the doctor here?'

'Who shall I say?'

But just then a window was opened wide. A jovial individual, with cards in his hand, leant out.

'Is it the bailiff's wife? I'm on my way.'

'A wounded man, doctor! Can you go straight away to the Hôtel de la Loire?'

'Not another crime, I hope?'

Three other people, gathered round a table shining with crystal glasses, got up. Maigret recognized Saint-Hilaire.

'Yes, a crime! Hurry!'

'Dead?'

'No! Take something for a dressing.'

Maigret never let his eyes stray from Saint Hilaire. He noticed that the owner of the 'little château' seemed very much upset.

'I have a question, gentlemen.'

'Wait a moment,' interrupted the notary. 'Why haven't you been let in?'

The servant, who had overheard, at last opened the door. The Chief Inspector walked down the passage and entered the drawing-room where the main impression was of a good smell of cigars and fine old brandy.

'What's happened?' inquired the host, who was an elderly man, well groomed, with soft hair and skin as clear as a baby's.

Maigret pretended not to have heard.

'I should like to know, gentlemen, how long you have been playing cards.' The notary glanced at the clock.

'A good hour . . .'

'Has any one of you left this room since then?'

They looked at each other in astonishment.

'Certainly not! There are only the four of us, just the number required for bridge.'

'You are absolutely sure of this?'

Saint-Hilaire was crimson in the face.

'Who's been attacked?' he asked, his throat dry.

'An employee of the Criminal Records office who was working in Émile Gallet's room; to be precise he was concerned with a certain Monsieur Jacob.'

'Monsieur Jacob . . .' repeated the notary.

'Do you know anyone of that name?'

'Good Heavens, no! It must be a Jew.'

'I have a favour to ask of you, Monsieur de Saint-Hilaire. I would like you to do your utmost to find the key of the gate. If necessary I can put some of my inspectors at your disposal to search the house.' Maigret took good note of the fact that the squire emptied his brandy glass in one gulp.

'Of course you'll have a drink with us, Chief Inspector?'

'Another time . . . Thank you . . .'

He set off again on the bicycle, turned to the left, and soon arrived at a rather dilapidated house with PENSION GERMAIN just decipherable on it. It was a poor-looking place of doubtful cleanliness. A grubby boy was crawling about on the doorstep, where a dog was gnawing a bone it had picked up in the dusty road.

'Is Mademoiselle Boursang here?'

A woman, holding another baby in her arms, came from the far end of a room.

'She has gone out, as she does every afternoon. . . . But most probably you will find her on the hill near the old château, because she took a book with her and it's her favourite spot.'

'Does this road take me there?'

'Turn to the right past the last house. . . .'

Half-way up the hill, Maigret had to get off and push the bicycle.

He was more nervous than he would have admitted, possibly because, once more, he had the feeling he was on the wrong track.

'It wasn't Saint-Hilaire who fired the shot, that's certain. And yet . . .'

The road he was following led through a kind of public garden. To the left on a sloping piece of land, a little girl was sitting beside three goats tethered to stakes.

There was a sharp bend in the road and just above him, a hundred yards off, Maigret saw Éléonore sitting on a bench, a book in her hand. He called to the little girl, who must have been about twelve years old.

'Do you know the lady sitting up there?'

'Yes, Monsieur.'

'Does she often come to read on that bench?'

'Yes, Monsieur.'

'Every day?'

'I think so, Monsieur. But when I go to school, I don't see her.'

'What time did you get here today?'

'Long time ago, Monsieur, I left as soon as I had had lunch.'

'And where do you live?'

'The house down there.'

It was a quarter of a mile away, a low-built house, partly farm buildings.

'Was the lady here when you came?'

'No, Monsieur!'

'When did she come?'

'I don't know, Monsieur! But it must be two hours ago anyway....'

'Did she go anywhere?'

'No, Monsieur.'

'Does she have a bicycle?'

'No, Monsieur.'

Maigret drew a two-franc piece from his pocket and put it in the girl's hand who clasped it without looking at it and remained motionless in the middle of the road, watching him while he climbed back on to his machine and set off for the village. He stopped at the Post Office and sent a telegram to Paris:

Wish to know all speed where Henri Gallet was Saturday three p.m. Maigret, Sancerre.

*

'Leave that, old chap!'

'You told me yourself it was urgent, Chief Inspector! Besides I don't feel anything now.'

Good old Moers! The doctor had put as thick and complicated a dressing on his wound as if he had had six bullets in the head. And the pince-nez with their shining lenses looked queer in the middle of all that white bandaging.

It was seven o'clock in the evening, and Maigret had not worried about him, knowing the wound was not serious; and now he found him again in the same place as in the morning, in front of his glass plates, his candle and spirit-stove.

'Although I haven't found anything further about Monsieur Jacob, I have just pieced together a letter signed by Clément, addressed to I don't know who, talking of a present to be given to an exiled prince. The word *obole* occurs twice and *loyalisme* once.'

'That's of minor importance. . . .'

Obviously that related to Gallet's swindling activities. Maigret had complete information on that subject from examination of the pink file, helped by a few telephone calls to various landowners in the Berry and Cher districts.

At some time not easy to determine exactly, possibly three or four years after his marriage, and a year or two after the death of his father-in-law, Émile Gallet had taken it into his head to make use of the old papers from *Soleil*, which he had inherited.

The paper, the product of Préjean's pen, had kept alive the hopes of a few country squires of seeing a Bourbon come back to the throne of France. Few copies had been printed, and they were reserved almost exclusively for the few regular subscribers.

Maigret had thumbed through the *Soleil* collection and had noticed that half a page was always devoted to subscription lists, whether for one of the old families which had fallen on bad days or for the propaganda funds, or even to finance suitable celebrations of some anniversary.

It was this which must have given Gallet the idea of swindling the Legitimists. He had their addresses, and even knew from these lists how much he might expect to screw out of them, and in each particular case what feelings to appeal to.

'Is it the same writing as on the other papers?'

'The same. My boss, Professor Locard, could tell you more. . . . . The writing is calm, careful, but with signs of nervousness and despondency in the word endings. . . . A handwriting expert would say straight away that the man who wrote these letters was ill, and knew it.'

'Good! That's enough for me, Moers. You can go and get a rest.'

Maigret was staring at the two holes in the blind – two holes made by the bullets.

'Go back for a moment to the spot where you were!'

He reconstructed the path of the bullets quite easily.

'The same angle,' he concluded. 'They came from the same place, from the top of the wall. . . . Hullo! What's that noise?'

He raised the blind, and saw the gardener raking about amongst the grass and nettles of the lane.

'What are you doing there?' Maigret called to him.

'My master told me . . .'

'To look for the key?'

'That's right!'

'And he sent you to this spot?'

'He's looking too, in the park; the cook and valet are searching the house. . . .'

With a quick movement Maigret lowered the blind and, alone with Moers again, he whistled softly: 'Well! Well! I'll bet you, old chap, he's the one who's going to find the key. . . .'

'What key?'

'It doesn't matter. It would take too long to explain. What time did you lower the blind?'

'As soon as I arrived, nearly half past one.'

'And you didn't hear footsteps in the lane?'

'I wasn't paying any attention – I was completely absorbed in this work I'm doing. It may seem idiotic, but it's really very tricky.'

'I know. I know. Now, who have I spoken to about Monsieur Jacob? The gardener, I think . . . And Saint-Hilaire, who went fishing, came back for lunch, dressed and went to his card-party. . . . Are you sure that all the other burnt papers were written by Monsieur Clément?'

'Absolutely certain.'

'Well, no matter . . . The only thing which counts is this letter signed by Monsieur Jacob, speaking of cash, of Monday, and seeming to demand twenty thousand francs on that day and threatening the recipient of the letter with imprisonment. The crime took place on Saturday.'

Every so often, outside, they could hear the rake hit against a stone.

'Neither Éléonore nor Saint-Hilaire fired, and yet . . .'

'Well, I never!' came the voice of the gardener suddenly.

Maigret smiled smugly and went to raise the blind.

'Give it to me!' he said, holding out his hand.

'If only I'd known it was here . . .'

'Give it to me!'

It was the key – an enormous key – of a kind only to be found now amongst antique dealers, and like the lock it was rusty and showed signs of scratches.

'Just tell your master that you've handed it over to me. . . . Go on!'

'Is it . . .'

'Go on!'

And Maigret let go the blind and threw the key on the table.

'Apart from your ear, you could say that this has been a very successful day, couldn't you, Moers? Monsieur Jacob . . . The key . . . The two shots, and all the rest! Ah, well! . . .'

'A telegram!' announced Monsieur Tardivon.

'What did I tell you, old chap?' concluded the Chief Inspector, after a glance at it. 'Instead of going forward, we go backwards. Listen to this! "*At three o'clock, Henri Gallet was with his mother in Saint-Fargeau. Was still there at six p.m.*"'

'So?'

'So, nothing! There's only Monsieur Jacob who could have fired at you, and up to now Monsieur Jacob has been just about as slippery as a cake of soap.'

CHAPTER 8

Monsieur Jacob

'HOLD on a minute, Aurore; there's no need to get in such a state. . . .'

And a muffled voice replied:

'I can't help it, Françoise . . . This visit reminds me of his other one a week ago. . . . And that journey! You just don't understand.'

'What I don't understand is that you can actually cry over a man like this, a man who brought disgrace on you, who lied all his life, and who did only one good thing – take out an insurance policy. . . .'

'Shut up!'

'What's more! He reduced you to a life almost of poverty and swore that he only earned 2,000 francs a month. The insurance proves that he earned twice that at least and was hiding it from you. For all we know then perhaps he earned even more. In my opinion if you want it, this man had two households, a mistress, and possibly some children somewhere. . . .'

'For pity's sake, Françoise!'

Maigret was alone in the little drawing-room at Saint-Fargeau, where the maid had shown him in and forgotten to close the door; so the two women's voices reached him from the dining-room, where the door was also ajar and opened into the same passage.

The furniture and smaller objects were back in their places and the Chief Inspector could not look at the large oak table without thinking that it had been covered in a black cloth, and bore a coffin and candles only a few days before.

It was a grey day; a heavy storm had broken during the night, but it felt as if there was more to come.

'Why should I be quiet? Do you think it's no concern o

mine? I am your sister; Jacques is just about to get an important position. Just imagine when the people of the district hear that his brother-in-law was a crook?'

'Then why did you come? You kept away for a good twenty years without ...'

'Without seeing you, because I didn't want to see him! When you wanted to marry him, I made no secret of what I thought, nor did Jacques! With the name of Aurore Préjean, with one brother-in-law director of one of the biggest tanneries in the Vosges and another who will one day be principal private secretary to a Minister of State, one doesn't marry an Émile Gallet! Not only the name, for heaven's sake – a commercial traveller too! I wonder how Father could have given his consent ... or perhaps, between ourselves, I can guess what happened ... Towards the end father only thought of one thing: whatever happened his magazine had to appear. Gallet had a little money.... It may be he was persuaded to put it in *Soleil*.... You can't tell me it's not true! But for you, a sister of mine, with the same education as me and with our mother's looks, to have chosen this nobody.... Don't look at me like that! I only want you to understand that there's no reason to cry.... Were you happy with him? Frankly ...'

'I don't know ... I don't know ...'

'You may as well admit you hoped for something better?'

'I always hoped that he would try something, I encouraged him to....'

'Might as well have encouraged a stone! And you put up with it! ... You didn't even know that when he died you wouldn't be a pauper.... Because, without the insurance ...'

'It was he who thought of it,' said Madame Gallet slowly.

'It's the least he could have done! Listening to you, I shall end up by believing you were in love with him....'

'Be quiet, the Inspector must have heard us.... I must go and speak to him....'

'What's he like? I'll come with you; in your present state it would be better ... But, Aurore, please don't look so shattered, the Inspector will think you were his accomplice; he will think that you are sad and afraid too.'

*

Maigret just had time to step back. The two women entered through the communicating door; they did not look as he had imagined from the conversation he had just overheard.

Madame Gallet was almost as distant as she had been at their first meeting. As for the sister, younger by two or three years, with her peroxide hair and made-up face, she gave the impression both of having more spirit and of putting on more airs.

'Have you any further news, Inspector?' asked the widow wearily. 'Please sit down. . . . This is my sister, who arrived yesterday from Épinal.'

'Where her husband is a tanner, I believe?'

'A tannery owner!' corrected Françoise dryly.

'Madame was not at the funeral? I see the newspapers reported three days ago that you will receive a life insurance of 300,000 francs,' he spoke softly, glancing right and left as if embarrassed. He had come to Saint-Fargeau with no definite object, to get the atmosphere again and get his picture of the dead man into focus once more.

He would have welcomed a meeting with Henri Gallet, though.

'I would like to ask you something!' he said, without turning towards the two women. 'Your husband must have known that your marriage to him cut you off from your family . . .'

It was Françoise who replied. 'That's not true, Inspector. At first we accepted him; many times, indeed, my husband advised him to look for another situation . . . he offered to help him. It was only when we saw that he would remain an inferior sort of person, incapable of effort all his life, that we avoided him. He would have put us to shame.'

'And you, Madame?' Maigret said softly, turning to Madame Gallet. 'Did you try to make him change his profession? Did you reproach him with it?'

'I should have thought this was a purely private matter. Had I any right to do so?'

Hearing her through the door a moment ago Maigret had imagined a woman whom sorrow had made more human and who had shed this haughty dignity; but it was just as on the first day, neither more nor less.

'Did your son get on well with his father?'

The sister charged in again.

'*Henri* will get somewhere! *He*'s a Préjean, though physically perhaps he is like his father. He did well to get out of this atmosphere when he came of age. . . . Only this morning, in spite of a liver attack the night before, he went back to work.'

Maigret was looking at the table, trying to picture Émile Gallet sitting somewhere in this room, but he did not succeed; perhaps because the people who lived in the house only used this room when there were visitors.

'Inspector, did you have something to tell me?'

'No. I shall leave you ladies with apologies for disturbing you. Oh, there is one thing! Have you a photograph of your husband taken when he was in Indo-China? He lived there, I believe, before his marriage?'

'I have no photographs. . . . My husband hardly ever spoke about that period of his life.'

'Do you know what he studied at school?'

'He was very well informed. . . . I remember him often discussing the Latin writers with my father.'

'But you don't know which school he went to when he was young?'

'All I know is that originally he came from Nantes.'

'Thank you. And once again, I beg your pardon.'

He collected his hat and backed out into the passage, unable to define the vague sense of uneasiness he felt every time he set foot in that house.

'I hope my name won't be bandied about in the newspapers, Inspector!' Françoise announced; her voice had more than a hint of impertinence. 'You may know that my husband is a

County Councillor – he has considerable influence in governmental circles and, as you are a public servant . . .'

Maigret could not bring himself to reply; he merely looked her straight in the eye and bowed himself out with a sign.

As he was going through the tiny garden, escorted by the squint-eyed maid, he muttered dreamily: 'Poor old Gallet!'

*

He merely looked in at the Quai des Orfèvres to get his mail, which contained nothing about the case. When he came out, he set off for the gunsmith's shop, where he hoped that the bullet extracted from the dead man's skull would have been examined, as well as the two aimed at Moers.

'Have you finished the report?'

'Yes. Just this moment. I was going to send it on. The three bullets were fired from the same weapon – there is no doubt about that. A precision-made, automatic revolver, current model, probably manufactured in the Herstal state factory.'

Maigret was dejected. He shook hands with the armourer and got into a taxi.

'Rue Clignancourt.'

'What number?'

'Put me down at the end of the street, doesn't matter which end.'

And on the way he tried to get rid of the clinging memory of the house at Saint-Fargeau, to put out of his mind the conversation between the two sisters, which haunted him, and to concentrate on the actual facts of the problem.

But as soon as he had got a few simple thoughts into order, Françoise would come back into his mind; Françoise, whose husband was a County Councillor – she hadn't forgotten to remind him of that. Oh, no! Françoise, who had made straight for Les Marguerites, when she heard that Madame Gallet was richer by three hundred thousand francs.

'*He was a disgrace to the family* . . .'

And right from the outset of his marriage, they had nagged

at Émile Gallet to ensure that he realized it was his duty to be a credit to the name of Préjean, like the other sons-in-law.

A commercial traveller in cheap presents! Yet he had had the courage to sign that life insurance and to pay the premium for a full five years! Maigret became almost lyrical about him, but at the same time he was worried, attracted and repelled by the dead man's complex make-up. Did he love his wife then, in spite of the fact that she must often have reproached him for the humble circumstances in which she lived?

A strange household! Strange lives! Just for a moment, and in spite of everything, had he not detected a spark of real affection in Madame Gallet? Admittedly she was the other side of a door. Once face-to-face with him that had been the end of it – she had once more become the unpleasant, pretentious little middle-class wife he had known on his first visit: a true sister of Françoise.

And Henri, who even on his way to his first communion, had something queer about him – thoughtful and distrustful. And who at the age of twenty-two would not marry Éléonore for fear of losing the pension she might get through her first husband! He had had a liver attack, but was back at work just the same!

It began to rain. The driver pulled up alongside the pavement to put up the hood of his taxi.

'The three bullets came from the same revolver. So it would be reasonable to suppose that they were fired by the same man! Now, neither Henri nor Éléonore nor Saint-Hilaire could have fired the last two shots. Nor a tramp! A tramp doesn't kill for the mere sake of killing: he steals – and nothing was stolen!'

The whole business of the inquiry, which revolved around the lifeless and melancholy face of the dead man, had become nauseating, and Maigret was in a grump when he entered the first concierge's little front room in the rue Clignancourt.

'Do you know a Monsieur Jacob?'

'What's he do?'

'I don't know. At any rate he gets letters in that name.'

The rain still came down in sheets, but the Chief Inspector welcomed it because in this weather the busy street, with its narrow shops and shabby houses, was all of a piece with his mood.

This pilgrimage from house to house could have been left to any junior constable, but Maigret was reluctant, he didn't know why, to get any of his colleagues into this case.

'Monsieur Jacob? ...'

'Not here ... Try next door; there are some Jews there.'

He had been into hundreds of *loges* or pushed his head through the little reception windows, questioning concierges by the hundred, when he came upon a large, fat woman with coarse flaxen hair who looked at him suspiciously.

'What d'you want with Monsieur Jacob? You're from the Police, aren't you?'

'Yes, Flying Squad. Is he at home?'

'You don't expect to find him in at this time, do you?'

'Where can I find him?'

'At his place, of course! At the corner of rue Clignancourt and Boulevard Rochechouart ... You're not going to make trouble for him, are you? A poor old man, who's never done any harm, I'm sure! Could be he hasn't got his permit.'

'Does he get much mail?'

The concierge frowned: 'It's for that, then!' she said. 'I thought there was something not quite right there! You should know as well as me, he gets just one letter every two or three months ...'

'Registered?'

'No. More like a little parcel than a letter.'

'Containing bank-notes?'

'I know nothing about that!' she replied dryly.

'Oh yes you do! You handled the envelope and you thought they were bank-notes too.'

'What of it then? Monsieur Jacob isn't the only one to run through bank-notes!'

'Where is his room?'

'His attic, do you mean? Right at the top! And it's pretty hard for him to take up all his things with those crutches of his.'

'Does no one ever ask for him?'

'Could be three years ago . . . a gentleman with a short beard; he looked like a parson in civvies. . . . I told him just what I'm telling you.'

'Was Monsieur Jacob getting letters by then?'

'He's just got one.'

'Did the man wear a morning-coat?'

'He was all in black, like a parson!'

'Does Monsieur Jacob ever have callers now?'

'No one except his daughter. She's a housemaid in a furnished flat in the rue Lepic, and she's going to have a baby.'

'What is his job?'

'What? You don't know? And you're a policeman? Are you kidding me by any chance? Monsieur Jacob, the oldest newspaper seller in the district; he's as well known as Methuselah. . . .'

Maigret stopped at the corner of rue Clignancourt and Boulevard Rochechouart in front of a bar with the name 'Au Couchant'. At the end of the café terrace was a man with a stall of roasted almonds and peanuts; in winter he probably sold chestnuts. On the Clignancourt side a little old man was sitting on a stool and repeating in a raucous voice, lost in the hubbub of the cross-roads:

'*Intran . . . Liberté . . . Presse . . . 'aris-Soir . . . Intran . . .*'

A pair of crutches rested against the front of the stall; there was a shoe on one foot, but the other boasted only a misshapen slipper. When he saw the news-seller, Maigret realized that Monsieur Jacob was not a name, but a nickname, for the old man had a long beard parted into two points, and above was a hooked nose just like those to be seen on the brand of clay pipes generally called 'Jacobs'.

The Chief Inspector remembered a few words from the

letter Moers had managed to piece together: *Twenty thousand* . . . *Numéra* . . . *Lundi* . . . and suddenly he bent down and put a question to the lame man:

'Have you got the last packet?' Monsieur Jacob raised his head, blinking his red-rimmed eyes. 'Who are you?' he asked at last, handing a copy of *L'Intransigeant* to a customer and hunting for change in a wooden bowl.

'Criminal Police. You'd better talk or I shall have to take you along with me. . . . It's a bad business. . . .'

'So what?'

'Have you a typewriter?'

The old man snorted and then spat out a chewed cigarette end of which he had quite a store in front of him. 'It's not worth your while playing smart with me!' he said, rolling his r's. 'You know very well it's not me! Anyhow I'd have done better to take it easy . . . for all I get out of it!'

'How much?'

'She gives me a hundred sous for each letter. . . . So it's a lousy business!'

'Enough to get those concerned into the Assize Courts.'

'No? Then they *did* contain thousand-franc notes. . . . I wasn't sure, I fingered the envelopes and they made a crackly sound. . . . I tried to look through them against the light, but the paper was too thick.'

'What was your part in it?'

'I brought the letters here. . . . I didn't even have to tell her in advance. . . . Near five o'clock I could be sure of the little lady coming; she would take a copy of *Intran*, put the hundred sous in the bowl, and slip the packet into her bag.'

'A little brunette . . .?'

'Not a bit! A tall blonde! A bit on the red side, well turned out, I'd say. She always came from the métro. . . .'

'When did she first ask you to do this for her?'

'Almost three years ago. . . Wait! Let's see, now! My daughter had just had her first baby and had taken him to a wet-nurse at Villeneuve-Saint-Georges. . . . Yes. That's just under three years ago. . . . It was late. . . . I had collected up the papers and was about to hoist them on my back. . . . She asked me if I had a home and if I'd help her. . . . You see, one meets all kinds here on this job.

'All I had to do was to receive letters addressed to me, not to open them, but bring them here in the afternoon.'

'Was it you who fixed the price of five francs?'

'She did. . . . I told her as a joke it was worth more than the price of a half-bottle of red wine, but then she was all for asking the peanut seller! An Algerian! Those people work for nothing! So I said yes. . . .'

'You don't know where she lives, I suppose?'

Monsieur Jacob winked. 'You'll be pretty smart if you find her, even though you're a policeman! There was one before who tried to find out. My concierge simply told him I was selling my papers here. She described him to me, and I thought he was the young lady's father. First of all he just hung around on the days when there was a packet, not speaking to me. Oh! And yes! He would hide over there behind the greengrocer's stall. Then he would chase after her. . . . Nothing doing, though! In the end he came to me and offered a thousand francs if I would give him the lady's address. He couldn't believe I didn't know it any more than he did. It turned out she had made him take I don't know how many métros and buses before shaking him off in some building with two exits.

'Not a nice guy, that. I realized he wasn't her father. . . . He tried his luck again twice. I thought I ought to warn my young lady and I'll bet she led him a pretty merry dance – several miles – because he didn't try it again. Well, there you are! D'you know what I got extra for that – instead of the thousand francs from the man? – Just a twenty-franc bit, and even then I had to pretend I hadn't any change or I'd only have got ten francs, and off she went muttering something very rude which I didn't understand. Sly little bitch! And a stingy old . . .!'

'When did the last letter come?'

'Three months ago at least . . . Can't you stand back a bit, customers can't see my papers now... Anything else you want to know? I'm a decent bloke, admit it, and I haven't tried to have you on....'

Maigret threw twenty francs into the bowl, made a vague gesture of farewell, and went off lost in thought.

Passing by the métro entrance, he pursed his lips with disgust at the idea of Éléonore Boursang going off with an envelope containing several thousand-franc notes, having thrown five francs to old Jacob, and then calmly boarding ten different métros and buses, and taking the extra precaution of going through a block of flats with two exits, before returning home. What connexion could this have with Émile Gallet taking off his coat and insisting on climbing a ten-foot wall?

Monsieur Jacob, Maigret's last hope, had vanished into thin air.

There was no such person as Monsieur Jacob! Must he now suppose that, instead, these two, Henri Gallet and Éléonore Boursang, had discovered Gallet's secret and were blackmailing him?

But Éléonore and Henri hadn't committed the murder; nor had Saint-Hilaire, in spite of his contradictory statements, in spite of the open gate and *the key he had himself thrown into Nettle Lane and which he arranged for his gardener to find after the Chief Inspector had declared that he would get his hands on it at all costs!*

This did not alter the fact that two bullets had been fired at Moers, and Émile Gallet, whose sister-in-law said he was a disgrace to the family, had been murdered.

The Saint-Fargeau lot consoled themselves by cursing him, by going on about him being a good-for-nothing with a low-class profession, and contemplating the fact that, after all, his death had made them richer by 300,000 francs.

Henri had got better that morning so that he could put his securities into Sovrino's Bank account and get full value for his 100,000 francs savings, which had to reach 500,000 before he could go and live in the country with Éléonore!

And she too, as calm as you please, swapping the packet for

a five-franc piece with the newspaper man, or watching Maigret's every movement at Sancerre, coming to him serene and innocent and telling him the story of her life!

And Saint-Hilaire had been playing cards at the notary's house. It was only Émile Gallet who was no longer on the scene. . . . He was firmly enclosed in a coffin, his cheek torn by the bullet, carved up by the police doctor with his seven people to dinner; a hole in his heart, and those grey eyes which no one had even thought of closing!

'Last path on the left, near that pink marble monument to the late mayor,' the verger in charge of the cemetery had said.

And the undertaker at Corbeil had scratched his head over an order specifying 'A very simple headstone, nothing elaborate, good taste, not too expensive, but distinguished'.

Maigret had seen others like it, and then he brought his mind back to thinking of a tall woman, with slightly red hair. It was not necessarily Éléonore Boursang, and, though she may have been Monsieur Jacob's client, nothing proved that Henri was her accomplice.

'The simplest thing to do would be to show a picture of her to the old man.' With this in mind he made his way to the Rue de Turenne, where he was pretty certain he would find a photograph of the young woman in her flat.

'Madame Boursang is not here, but Monsieur Henri is upstairs,' said the concierge.

Evening was falling; Maigret stumbled against the walls of the narrow staircase, and, without knocking, opened the door which she had pointed out to him.

Henri Gallet was bent over the table, tying up a rather bulky parcel. He jumped, but managed to get a grip of himself when he recognized the Chief Inspector. However, he couldn't get a word out. He was clenching his teeth so hard they must have ached. There had been a horrifying change in him in one short week. His cheeks were hollow with the cheek-bones sticking out. Above all, his complexion was a fearful ashen colour.

'It seems that last night you had a terrible liver attack,' said

Maigret with a brusqueness he didn't mean. 'Out of the way ...'

The parcel looked like a typewriter. The detective tore off the wrapping, looked for a sheet of white paper in his pocket, and typed several words at random. Then he slipped the paper into his wallet.

For a moment the noise of the machine had broken the silence in the flat, where dust-sheets covered the furniture and newspapers were stuck on the window-panes over the holidays. Henri, leaning against a chest of drawers, was looking down at the floor, so tense that he was painful to look at.

Maigret carried on with his job ponderously and relentlessly, opening drawers and rummaging about amongst the contents. Finally he came on a picture of Éléonore.

Then, just as he was about to leave, hat on the back of his head, photograph in hand, he stopped for a moment in front of the young man and looked him up and down.

'You've nothing to tell me?'

Henri swallowed and managed to get out: 'Nothing.'

*

Maigret was careful not to get to the rue Clignancourt for an hour. Monsieur Jacob was still sitting beside his papers.

Was any more proof wanted? Before coming up with the old man, he had caught sight of Henri Gallet's long, pale face through the window of a bar.

A moment later, Monsieur Jacob was saying: 'That's her, all right! No doubt about it. Now she's done for!'

Maigret went off without a word, and with a baleful glance at the bar. He could have gone in and started another liver attack by merely putting his hand on Henri's shoulder.

'The fact remains, *they* did not kill him!'

Half an hour later, he was in Police Headquarters; he spoke to no one; on his desk he found a letter from the Inspector of Taxes at Nevers.

CHAPTER 9

A Fake Marriage

If you should care to pay a discreet visit to my private address, number 17 rue Creuse, Nevers, I will give you information on Emile Gallet which should be of great interest to you.

Maigret was in the rue Creuse.

Opposite him, in a red and black drawing-room, was the Inspector of Taxes, who had let him in himself with the air of a conspirator.

'I have sent the maid off. You understand? It's better like that, you know. And as far as anybody who may have seen you come in goes, you are my cousin from Beaucaire.'

Was he winking at Maigret in order to give force to his words? At all events, instead of closing one eye, he closed them both, quickly, ending by giving the impression that he had a nervous tic.

'Were you once in the colonies, like me? ... No? I should have thought ... Pity, because you would understand better. ...'

His eyelids opened and closed all the time; his tone of voice became more and more confidential, and in his expression were both malice and fear.

'I was ten years in Indo-China myself; there were no great boulevards in Saigon then, like in Paris. ... It was there I got to know Gallet. ...

'And what put me on the scent was the knifing. ... You will see why very soon.

'You've found nothing, I bet! You will find nothing, because it's a story only a colonial could understand. And even then, a colonial who was present *when it happened*.'

Maigret had by now sized up his man; he knew that with this sort one had to conceal any impatience, refrain from interrupting, and nod one's approval; otherwise the waste of time would be incalculable!

'He was a great chap, our Gallet! He acted as a sort of notary's clerk, to a man who has since got on in life, for he became a senator.... Mad on sport. He even put forward the idea of forming a football team.... He got after us all in a big way, but as there was no other team to play against us... Well, to cut a long story short... He liked his women even more than football.... And there you can have them for the asking.... A gay dog! The tricks he was able to play on them...

'Just a moment please...'

He crept to the door and suddenly wrenched it open to see if anyone were listening.

'Well, now... Once he went a bit too far, and I am not proud of having played the part of accomplice, though – mind – without getting mixed up in it myself.... A planter had just brought across two or three hundred Malay workers.... Amongst the gang were some women and children and a little creature who was a real peach!... I don't remember her name now.

'On the other hand, I remember I was finishing an old book of Stevenson's about natives in the Pacific, which I had talked to Gallet about. It's about a white man who organizes a fake marriage, to get a real wild native girl....

'Well, there's my Émile well and truly carried away! At that time the Malays were still illiterate, especially the poorer ones, who were carted around like cattle....

'Well, Gallet goes off to ask the girl's father for her.... He rigged out his future in-laws in ridiculous clothes and organized a complete procession to an old hut we had already marked down.

'The fellow who acted the part of the mayor has since died, but you could find others who took part in the act. Gallet was an awful practical-joker! He had forgotten nothing that could make this a real comedy. The speeches were so funny we were practically rolling on the ground with laughter – and the whole marriage ceremony, which the girl was solemnly made to go through – it was daft from start to finish! . . . It was the biggest joke of all! And the whole family were taken in, witnesses and everyone else. . . .'

The tax inspector was silent for a moment, just long enough to put on a more serious expression.

'Well,' he concluded, 'Gallet lived with her as man and wife for three or four months. Then he went back to France and, naturally, he left his "wife" behind.

'We were young then, otherwise we would not have laughed so much, because the Malays do not forgive.

'You don't know them, Inspector. The young girl waited a long time for her husband to come back. . . . I don't know what happened to him afterwards, but a few years later, I met her, looking much older, in a very seamy quarter of Saigon. . . .

'When I read the name Gallet in the Nevers paper . . . Remember I haven't seen him for twenty-five years. I haven't even heard about him. . . . It's the knifing, you see? Now, have you guessed. Vengeance, obviously! These Malays will go right round the world for revenge. . . . And they use the dagger. . . .

'Imagine a brother or even a son of the little girl. . . . More civilized. He began using a revolver, because it's more practical. Then his instincts took over. . . .'

Maigret waited gloomily, only half listening to this torrent of words which it was useless to interrupt. Usually in a criminal case there are hundreds of witnesses of this man's sort.

If it hadn't been this one it would have been another, because the Paris newspapers had reported the affair quite extensively.

'Are you with me, Inspector? You would never have guessed, now, would you? I preferred to ask you to come here because if the murderer were to know I had talked . . .'

'You said Gallet played football?'

'A fabulous player! And a jolly fine fellow! The most

amusing companion you could ask for . . . He could tell funny stories the whole evening without drawing breath.'

'Why did he leave Indo-China?'

'He used to say he had his own ideas and wasn't born to live with less than 100,000 francs for a pension. . . . This was before the war. A pension of 100,000 francs! Can you see it! We made fun of him, but he was as solemn as a pope. . . . You'll see! You'll see! He would laugh. He didn't get his 100,000 francs, did he? With me, it was the fever chased me out of Asia. . . . I still have bouts of it now. Would you like something to drink, Inspector? I shall get it for you myself, as I've sent the maid out for the afternoon.'

No, Maigret couldn't face anything, nor could he put up further with the man's childish winking as he told his tale of Malay vengeance.

He could hardly bring himself to say thank you or to smile a watery smile, purely out of politeness.

Two hours later he was getting off the train at Tracy-Sancerre station, where he was already beginning to feel at home. And on the road to the Hôtel de la Loire he soliloquized:

'Suppose it's Saturday, 25 June. . . . I am Émile Gallet. The heat is overpowering . . . my liver is giving trouble. . . . And I have a letter from Monsieur Jacob in my pocket, threatening to reveal everything to the police if I don't hand over 20,000 francs in cash to him by Monday.

'The Legitimists never subscribe 20,000 francs in one go. The average sum you can squeeze out of them varies between 200 and 600 francs. Rarely 1,000. *At the Hôtel de la Loire I ask for a room overlooking the yard. . . .*

'Why the yard? Am I afraid of being murdered? Who by?'

He walked, head bent, slowly, making a real effort to put himself in the dead man's place.

'Do I know who Monsieur Jacob really is? He has blackmailed me for three years. I questioned the newspaper-seller on the corner of the rue Clignancourt. . . . I followed a young blonde, who left me in the lurch in front of a building with two exits. . . . No good thinking it's Henri; I don't know anything about his mistress. And I don't know that he has already amassed 100,000 francs, or that he needs half a million to be able to go and live in the Midi. Monsieur Jacob, therefore, is still someone fearfully well camouflaged as an old newsvendor.'

He made a movement like a schoolteacher wiping off with a duster a problem chalked on the black-board.

He would have liked to forget all the evidence and start the investigation over again from A to Z.

'*Émile Gallet was a gay young fellow! He dragooned his friends into forming a football team. . . .*'

He passed the hotel without going in, and rang at the nain entrance to Saint-Hilaire's property. Monsieur Tardivon, vho was standing at the hotel porch and to whom Maigret ad not said good day, gazed after him reproachfully.

The Chief Inspector had to wait some time in the street. At ast a man-servant came to let him in, and Maigret asked pointlank:

'How long have you been in this house?'

'A year . . . But . . . it must be Monsieur de Saint-Hilaire hat you wish to see?'

His master gave Maigret a friendly wave from a groundloor window.

'Well! That key? We had it after all! Will you come in a econd? And how go the investigations?'

'How long has your gardener been with you?'

'Three or four years . . . Won't you come in?'

The squire was struck by the change which had come over Aaigret; his face was set and frowning, and when he looked at ou his expression was worrying; he looked tired and spiteful.

'I'll get a bottle brought up. . . .'

'What became of the old gardener?'

'He keeps a bar, a mile from here on the Saint-Thibaut road. . . An old rascal, who made his pile with me before settling lown on his own. . . .'

'Thank you.'

'Are you going?'

'I'll be back....'

He said it without thinking; he arrived at the postern-gate still worried and moved off in the direction of the main road.

'He had to have 20,000 francs immediately! He didn't try to get it from his usual victims, in other words the landowners in the neighbourhood. He went *only* to Saint-Hilaire.... *Twice* in the same day ... Then he climbed on to the wall!' He broke off with an oath.

'Damn! damn! damn! But, in that case, why did he ask for a room *overlooking the yard*? If he had got it, he wouldn't have been able to climb the wall.'

The old gardener's inn stood near the lock of the Loire cana and was swarming with bargees.

'Could you give me a bit of information please.... Police ... About the crime at Sancerre ... Do you ever remember seeing Émile Gallet at your former employer's when you were there?'

'You mean Monsieur Clément? ... That's what we called him.... Yes, I saw him.'

'Often?'

'I wouldn't like to say.... Let's say every six months... But it was enough to put the old man in a bad way for a fort night!'

'His first visits were a long time back?'

'At least ten years. Perhaps fifteen. Will you have a glass of something?'

'No thanks ... Did they sometimes quarrel?'

'Not sometimes – every time! And I even saw them go for each other like a couple of dockers....'

And yet it wasn't Saint-Hilaire who had fired, reasoned Maigret to himself a little later, on his way back to the hotel First, he could not have fired the two shots at Moers, since he was at the notary's. Secondly, on the night of the crime, why would he have gone round by the gate?

He caught sight of Éléonore, not far from the church, but looked the other way to avoid her. He didn't feel like talking, least of all to her.

He heard hurried steps behind him. He saw her come up with him, in a grey dress, her hair very sleek.

'Excuse me, Inspector . . .'

He turned and looked her in the eye with such a baleful expression that she caught her breath for a moment.

'Well?'

'I just wanted to know . . .'

'There's nothing to know, I know nothing at all. . . .'

And he moved off without another word, his hands behind his back.

'If the room overlooking the yard had been free . . . would he have died just the same?'

A child playing with a ball bumped into him; he lifted him up and put him down a yard farther on without even looking at him.

'Anyway, he didn't have the 20,000 francs. . . . He couldn't get them by Monday. . . .'

And he would not have been able to climb the wall! From the wall, it would have been impossible to shoot him.

Therefore, *he would not have been dead*!

He mopped his brow, though the weather was very much more bearable than the week before.

He had the maddening feeling of being within an ace of his goal, and yet unable to get there. There was plenty of evidence; the wall for one, the two shots fired at Moers, a week later the Jacob business, the visits made fifteen years ago to Saint-Hilaire, the lost key, so providentially found by the gardener, the question of rooms, the knife-wound completing the work of the bullet a few seconds later, and finally the football and the marriage farce. Gallet's passion for sport, his funny stories and amorous adventures were all he had got out of the tax inspector's involved stories.

'A gay dog! A great Don Juan!'

'Will you dine on the terrace, Inspector?' asked Monsieur Tardivon. Maigret had arrived at the hotel without realizing it.

'I don't mind.'

'Well? This investigation?'

'One might say it's over. . . .'

'What? And the murderer?'

But the detective moved off, shrugging his shoulders, along the corridors filled with smells from the kitchen, and went into the room where his papers were still piled on the table, on the mantelpiece, and on the floor.

The clothes representing the dead man had not been touched.

Maigret leaned over, pulled out the knife he had stuck in the wooden floor-boards, and began to finger it, walking up and down all the time.

The sky was overcast with an unbroken layer of grey storm-clouds, and in contrast the white wall opposite was dazzling. The Chief Inspector paced from window to door, from door to window, glancing every now and again at the photograph on the mantelpiece.

'Come here a moment!' he said suddenly, as he reached the window for about the thirtieth time.

The leaves above the wall shook at the spot where Maigret had spotted Saint-Hilaire's half-hidden face. The squire's first inclination was to make off, but then, trying to make a joke of it, he asked in an agitated voice:

'Must I jump?'

'Go round by the gate, it's easier!'

The key was on the table; Maigret threw it carelessly over the wall and went on pacing up and down the room. He heard the key fall in the park, among the rubbish piled up there. Then there was the noise of the barrel being shifted and again a rustling of leaves and branches. Saint-Hilaire's hand must have been trembling, because the key rattled in the lock for some time before the sound of the grating hinges came.

However, by the time the owner of the 'little château' had appeared at the window, he had recovered his poise and he said playfully:

'Can't escape your lynx-like eye! . . . This case fascinates me so much that seeing you come back gave me the idea of watching you, so that I should know as much about it as you, and lure you to another meeting. . . . Shall I go round?'

'No, don't. Climb through the window. . . .'

Saint-Hilaire did so without difficulty, and looking round said:

'How odd! . . . All this atmosphere, all this business of reconstructing the facts . . . These clothes . . . Did you organize this stage-set?'

Maigret filled his pipe with exaggerated deliberation, packing in each screw of tobacco with his index finger a dozen times.

'Have you a light?'

'A lighter . . . I never use matches. . . .'

The Chief Inspector's eye seemed to rest on three bits of greenish wood, burnt at the ends, lying in the hearth near the burnt paper. 'Of course!' he said. But there was no knowing to whom this comment was addressed.

'You wanted to ask me something?'

'I don't know yet; I saw you . . . and, as I am still totally in the dark, I said to myself that an intelligent man might be able to give me some ideas. . . .' He sat down on a corner of the table and held the bowl of his pipe toward the lighter held by his companion.

'Hullo! You're left-handed. . . .'

'What? Me? . . . No! It's just chance. Couldn't possibly tell you why I held the lighter out to you with my left hand. . . .'

'Would you mind closing the window? I'd be very grateful . . .'

Maigret's eyes never left him; he noticed Saint-Hilaire hesitate a moment, and then, obviously thinking hard, he used his right hand to turn the clasp of the window.

CHAPTER 10

The Assistant

'OPEN the window!'

'But you've just asked me to ...' and Tiburce de Saint-Hilaire smiled as if to say: 'All right, you're giving the orders. ... However, I don't quite understand.'

But Maigret was not smiling. Anyone looking at him would have said it was primarily boredom which showed in his face. He acted and spoke as if in a grumpy mood. He moved jerkily and jerked his head up and down, or took something up and put it down elsewhere for no apparent reason.

'Since this investigation fascinates you, I'll take you on as my assistant. ... So no kid gloves, and I shall treat you as one of my inspectors. ... Call the landlord.'

Saint-Hilaire obediently opened the door and shouted: 'Tardivon! Hey! Tardivon! ...'

When the hotel proprietor came in, Maigret was sitting on the window-ledge, staring at the floor.

'A simple question, Monsieur Tardivon ... Was Gallet left-handed? Try to remember. ...'

'I never noticed. ... It's true that ... Does a left-handed man shake hands with his left hand?'

'Of course.'

'Then he wasn't, because I'd have noticed that. ... Usually the visitors shake hands with me. ...'

'Go and ask the staff. ... Perhaps they noticed.'

When he was gone, Saint-Hilaire asked:

'You attach great importance to this question of ...?'

But the Chief Inspector, without replying, went out into the passage and called out to the manager:

'At the same time, will you get me Monsieur Padailhan, the tax inspector in Nevers. ... I think he's on the telephone. ...'

He came back into the room without looking at his companion and walked round the clothing spread out on the floor.

'Now to work! Let's see. . . . Émile Gallet was not left-handed. We'll soon see whether this fact will help us . . . or rather . . . take this knife. . . . It was the one used for the crime. . . . No. Give it to me, because there you go again using your left hand.'

'There. Now let us suppose that I am being attacked and therefore must fight back. And I am not left-handed, remember. Of course, I hold the handle of the knife in my right hand. . . . Come here. . . . I charge at you. . . . You are stronger than me. . . . You seize my wrist. . . . Seize hold of it! Good! It's obvious that you're going to get hold of the hand with the weapon in it. Good enough. Now look at this photograph. It's of the body, taken by the Criminal Records office. Now what do you see? That Émile Gallet's left wrist is bruised.

'Yes, Tardivon? Nevers already? No? You say that the waitresses all agree that Gallet was not left-handed? Thank you. You may go. . . .

'Between ourselves, Monsieur de Saint-Hilaire . . . How do *you* explain this?

'Gallet was not left-handed, and yet it was with the left hand he held the weapon! If you consider the evidence it proves that there was nothing in his right hand. . . .

'I see only one solution to the puzzle. . . . Look . . . I want to plunge this knife into my heart. . . . What do I do? Follow every movement. . . .

'I take the handle in my left hand. Because this hand is only going to be used to guide the knife in the right direction . . . My right hand is the stronger. . . . It's with that one I put pressure on the left. . . . Wait! Like this . . . My right hand grasps my left wrist. . . . I squeeze very hard because I am wrought up and know it's going to hurt. . . . I squeeze so hard that I bruise myself.'

He threw the knife casually back on the table.

'Of course, if you accept this reconstruction of the facts, you also accept that Gallet committed suicide. . . . But then his arm wasn't long enough to hold a revolver twenty feet away from his face, was it?

'*As you were*, as they say in the Army. Let us think of something else!'

Saint-Hilaire was still smiling rather wanly. But his eyes were staring, and they shifted back and forth continually, so as never to leave Maigret, who was pacing up and down all the time, making fifty meaningless motions where one would have done, taking up the pink file, opening it, closing it again, sliding it under the green file, and suddenly going to change the position of one of the dead man's shoes. . . .

'Come with me. . . . Yes, out of the window . . . Here we are in Nettle Lane. . . . Let us imagine it is Saturday evening, it is night, and we can hear the noise of the fair and the shooting-gallery. . . . Perhaps we can even see the flickering lights of the merry-go-round.

'Émile Gallet had taken off his coat; he hoists himself to the top of the wall, which is not an easy thing for a man of his age and with his strength undermined by ill health. . . .

'Follow me.'

He led him along to the gate, opened it, and closed it again.

'Give me the key. . . . Good . . . This gate was closed and the key was usually in the crack between those two stones there . . . your gardener himself told me . . . and now we are in your property. . . . Don't forget it's dark. . . . Remember we are only trying to make sense of certain pieces of evidence, or rather, we are trying to make certain contradictory pieces of evidence fit. . . .

'This way please! Let us imagine now, in the park, someone who is worried by what Émile Gallet is doing . . . there must be quite a few who are . . . Gallet is a swindler . . . God knows what else he has got to answer for.

'On this side of the wall, then, there is a man, like you or me, who noticed that Gallet was nervous that evening and perhaps knew that he was in a desperate situation.... Our man, whom we shall name *X* as in algebra, walks up and down by the wall and suddenly sees the silhouette of Émile Gallet, alias Monsieur Clément, appear on top of the wall, coatless. Can you see this bit of the wall from the house?'

'No ... I don't understand what you ...'

'What I'm driving at? I'm not driving at anything. We are merely carrying on the investigation and we may alter our hypothesis a hundred times if necessary.... Wait! I've changed it already! *X* is not walking up and down.... He saw the empty barrels and, rather than climb over the wall to find out what is going on on the other side, he dragged one of the barrels over and used it to stand on.

'It is at this moment that Émile Gallet's silhouette stands out against the sky....

'The two do not speak, because if they had had something to say they would have got closer to each other. You have to talk quite loud to hear over a distance of thirty feet.... And people who meet in such peculiar circumstances, one on a barrel, the other balancing on a wall, do not want to attract attention. ... Besides, *X* is in the shadow, Émile Gallet does not see him, comes down from his perch, returns to his room, and ...

'Here, it becomes more difficult, unless we assume it was *X* who fired....'

'What do you mean?'

Maigret, who had climbed on to the barrel, got down heavily.

'Give me a light. Good. Your left hand again! Now without bothering about who fired we are going to follow the route our *X* took.... Come ... He takes the key from its place.... He opens the gate.... Beforehand, however, he went somewhere and got some rubber gloves.... You'll have to ask your cook if she wears them for peeling vegetables and whether they have disappeared.... Is she tidy-minded?'

'I don't see the point....'

A distant roll of thunder could be heard, but not a drop of rain fell.

'Let's go through! The gate is open now, *X* comes to the window and sees the body.... You see, Émile Gallet is dead! ... The knife was used *immediately* after the shot was fired, the doctors say so quite positively and the traces of blood prove it.... Now, we saw earlier that this stabbing had all the appearances of being done by the victim himself....

'In the hearth there are some charred bits of paper, still warm, and we find Gallet's matches there too....

'This *X*, however, rummages in the suitcase, probably also in the wallet, which he carefully puts back in the pocket, and goes off, forgetting to close the gate and put the key back in its place....

'However, the key is rediscovered in the grass....'

Maigret, who had not glanced at his companion for some time, noticed that he looked disconcerted.

'Now then ... That's not all. I don't think I have ever come across a case that was so complicated and at the same time so simple.... We know, don't we, that the man who called himself Clément here was a crook.... Now, we find that he destroyed all traces of his fraud himself, as though he were expecting something important, something decisive to happen.

'This way! Here is the hotel yard, and there, to the left, the room which Émile Gallet asked for that afternoon and which they couldn't give him as it wasn't free....

'Now, in the afternoon his situation was the same as in the evening. He must whatever happens have 20,000 francs by Monday morning, otherwise his blackmailers would hand him over to the police....

'Suppose he had got this room.... There wouldn't have been any way of crossing over Nettle Lane and climbing on to the wall!

'Therefore, getting on to the wall for him wasn't an essential, or put another way, something else could take its place, something which the yard could provide.

'What do we see in this yard? A well! Perhaps you will tell me he wanted to throw himself in.... But to that I would reply that he could drown himself quite easily by leaving his room, crossing the passage, and getting out that way. . . .

'No! he had to have both a well and a room together.'

'Yes, Monsieur Tardivon?'

'Nevers on the line. . . .'

'The tax inspector?'

'Yes . . .'

'Come, Monsieur de Saint-Hilaire. . . . Since you want to help me, it is right that you should be there at every stage of this investigation. . . . Take the other earphone! . . . Hullo! Chief Inspector Maigret here. . . . Nothing to be afraid of. I just want to ask you one question which crossed my mind a moment ago. . . . Your friend Gallet . . . was he left-handed? What did you say? . . . Left-handed and left-footed? At football he played outside left? Are you quite sure? No. That's all, thank you. . . . One small point: did he know Latin? Why do you laugh? A dunce? As bad as that? Odd, isn't it? Tell me – have you seen a photograph of the dead man? No? Obviously, he has changed since the Saigon days. . . . The only picture I have was taken when he was on a diet. . . . But perhaps one of these days I'll introduce you to someone who looks very much like him. . . . Thank you. Yes! . . .'

Maigret hung up, gave a singularly mirthless laugh, and sighed: 'You see how wrong one can get when carried away? All that we have said so far rests on one supposition, that the Émile Gallet we are dealing with was not left-handed. . . . Because if he had been he could have used the knife on his attacker. . . . You see what it is to put any faith in the statements of hotel managers and waitresses. . . .'

Monsieur Tardivon, who had heard, looked prim.

'Dinner is served.'

'In a moment, almost finished, particularly as I'm afraid I must be trying Monsieur de Saint-Hilaire's patience. Let's go back to the scene of the crime, as they say, do you mind?'

*

When they got there, he said suddenly:

'You have seen Émile Gallet alive. . . . What I am going to say may perhaps make you laugh. . . . Yes. Do put on the light; with this foul weather it gets dark an hour earlier than usual. . . . Well, I didn't see him, and I have spent all my time since the crime trying to imagine him alive. . . .

'To do that, I want to breathe the air he breathed . . . rub shoulders with the people he lived with. . . . Look at this picture. . . . I bet you'll say the same as I did: "Poor fellow!" Especially when you know that the doctors gave him only three more years to live. A rotten liver . . . And a tired heart just waiting for an excuse to stop . . . I want to picture this man as a living being, not only in space but in time. . . . Unfortunately I could only go as far back as his marriage; he wouldn't ever tell even his wife what happened before that. . . . All that she knows is that he was born in Nantes and that he lived several years in Indo-China. But he didn't bring back a photograph or a souvenir. He never spoke about it. . . .

'He was a little commercial traveller, with some thirty thousand francs. . . . Even at the age of thirty he was skinny, awkward, with a melancholy disposition.

'He met Aurore Préjean and decided to marry her. . . . The Préjeans are social climbers. . . . The father was hard pressed and no longer had enough money to keep his paper alive. . . . But he had been the private secretary to a pretender to the throne! He had corresponded with dukes and princes!

'His eldest girl married a master tanner.

'Gallet cut a miserable figure in that society, and if he was accepted at all it was only because he agreed to put his little bit of capital into the *Soleil* business. . . . They didn't put up with him easily. For the Préjeans it's a come-down that a son-in-law should sell silver-plate articles for cheap presents.

'They try to give him a bit more ambition. . . . He resists. He's not made for a great career. His liver is far from good at that time. . . . He dreams of a peaceful life in the country with his wife, of whom he is very fond.

'But she nags at him too! Her sisters even have the audacity to treat her as a poor relation and hold her marriage up against her.

'Préjean dies.... *Soleil* founders. Émile Gallet continues to sell his tawdry knick-knacks as gifts for Normandy peasants...

'After this he consoles himself by fishing, by inventing fishing gadgets and taking alarm-clocks and watches to pieces.

'His son inherits from him his physique and his liver trouble, but he has the ambition of the Préjeans. And so one fine day Émile Gallet decides to try out something.... He has the files of *Soleil*. He discovers that a lot of people have forked out quite considerable sums of money as soon as someone talked to them of the Legitimist cause.

'He has a shot.... He says nothing about it.... Perhaps, at first, he carries on his business as commercial traveller and starts his swindling in a small way only.

'The swindling does better than his business. Soon he can buy a site on the Saint-Fargeau development estate; he builds a house there....

'He applies his qualities of orderliness and punctuality to his new occupation. Since he is mortally afraid of his family he continues, as far as they are concerned, to represent Niel and Company in Normandy.

'He does not make a fortune. Legitimists don't come by the million. Some of them are close-fisted with their money.... But at any rate it's a comfortable little income, on which Gallet can be happy as long as no one reproaches him, even under his own roof, with having little or no ambition.

'He is fond of his wife, in spite of all her faults. Perhaps he was even fond of his son....

'The years go by.... His liver gets worse.... Gallet has attacks, and they make him feel he hasn't long to live.

'Then he takes out a life-insurance at a premium high enough to ensure that his dependants can maintain their same standard of living after his death. He wears himself out.... Monsieur Clément visits the manor houses in the provinces more and more frequently, hounding the dowagers and gentlemen of the old régime.

'Do you follow me?

'Now, after three years, a Monsieur Jacob writes to him. This Monsieur Jacob knows the nature of his business and demands money, every two months, in a continuous stream, for the price of his silence. . . .

'What can Gallet do? He is a disgrace to the Préjean family – the poor relation; they don't mind sending him a card at New Year, but his brothers-in-law, who have their careers to think of, prefer not to meet him.

'On Saturday, 25 June, he is here, with Monsieur Jacob's last letter in his pocket, demanding twenty thousand francs by the following Monday. . . .

'I went over the route from the station to the hotel, not long ago, trying to put myself in his shoes.

'It's obvious that you can't collect twenty thousand francs in one day by knocking on Legitimists' doors, even on the most ingenious of pretexts. At any rate, he doesn't try. He calls on you – twice! After his second interview with you, he asks for a room overlooking the yard.

'Did he hope to get the twenty thousand out of you? Whatever happened, the fact remains that by the evening that hope was gone. Now, if you can tell me what it was he wanted to do in the room he didn't get, then we shall know why he climbed on to the wall!'

Maigret didn't raise his eyes towards his companion, whose lips were trembling.

'It's ingenious . . . Very . . . Especially the bits about me. I don't quite see?'

'How old were you when your father died?'

'Twelve.'

'Is your mother still alive?'

'She died soon after I was born. . . . But I would like to know why . . .'

'Were you brought up by relatives?'

'I had no relatives. I am the last of the Saint-Hilaires. There was just enough money, after my father had died, to pay for my board and education in a college in Bourges until I was nineteen. If it hadn't been for an unexpected legacy from a cousin whom everybody had forgotten the existence of . . .'

'And who lived in Indo-China, I believe?'

'Yes, somewhere there . . . He was a second cousin not even of the same name. A Duranty de la Roche . . .'

'When did you inherit this?'

'When I was twenty-eight . . .'

'So that from the age of eighteen to twenty-eight . . .?'

'I had a tough time of it, I can tell you! I'm not ashamed of it. On the contrary! It's late, Inspector – I think it might be a good thing if . . .'

'One moment, I haven't yet shown you what can be done with a well and a room. Have you got a gun on you? Doesn't matter, I have mine. . . . There must be some string somewhere. Good. Follow me closely. I tie the string to the handle of the weapon. Let's say it's six to seven yards long, or a bit more, doesn't matter. . . . Go and fetch a large stone from the road. . . .'

Once again Saint-Hilaire obeyed with alacrity and brought back a stone.

'With the left hand!' remarked Maigret. 'Never mind. Now, I tie the stone securely to the other end of the string. . . . We can try this out here if we imagine the window-ledge to be the lip of the well. . . .

'I let the stone down the other side. Into the well it goes. My revolver is in my hand. . . . I shoot at somebody, anybody – myself for instance. . . . Then I let go. What happens? The stone, which is hanging over the water, sinks to the bottom of the well, taking with it the revolver which is tied to the other end of the string.

'The police arrive, find a corpse, but no trace of a weapon. . . . What do they conclude?'

'A crime!'

'Very good!'

And Maigret lit his pipe with matches he took from his pocket; he had no need to ask for his companion's lighter now.

Whilst collecting up Gallet's clothes, like a man relieved to have finished a long and difficult task, he said in a perfectly natural voice: 'Now go and fetch the revolver.'

'But – You've got it in your hand – you didn't let it go.'

'What I mean is, go and fetch me the revolver which killed Gallet. Hurry up!'

And he hung the trousers and waistcoat on the peg beside the coat which was hanging there already, its elbows worn and shiny.

CHAPTER 11

A Business Transaction

As Maigret turned his back on him, Saint-Hilaire no longer had to conceal his true feelings; and a curious mixture appeared in his face, fear, hatred, but in spite of it all – a certain self-assurance.

'What are you waiting for?'

He made up his mind to go through the window, walked up to the gate in Nettle Lane, and disappeared into the park; it was all done so slowly that the Chief Inspector was a little worried and listened to see whether he could catch a sound.

This was the time of day when a glow of light from the terrace became visible in the direction of the embankment and the clatter of knives and forks could be heard to the accompaniment of the subdued murmur of the hotel visitors' conversation.

Suddenly the branches moved on the other side of the wall. It was so dark that Maigret could hardly make out Saint-Hilaire's figure on the top.

Again a snapping of branches . . . A soft call came:

'Will you take it?'

The Chief Inspector shrugged his shoulders and did not move so that the other had to come the whole way back.

When he was inside he put the weapon on the table straight away. He seemed quite calm. He was standing up straight, and he touched Maigret's arm almost jauntily though obviously somewhat embarrassed.

'What would you say to 200,000?'

He coughed nervously.

He had wanted to give the impression of the Great Man, very much at ease – and here he was going red in the face and with a choke in his throat.

'Well, I could make it 300 perhaps. . . .'

Maigret looked at him without emotion, without anger, but with a little touch of sarcasm in his heavy-lidded eyes; he lost his nerve, and stepped back, glanced round the room as if to find something to hold on to. It was a quick change; all he could manage was a vulgar smile, and even so his face was going brick red, and his eyes flashing with anxiety.

His Great Man role had not been a success. He tried another tactic, cynical, more down to earth!

'That's on you! Perhaps I was a bit naïve anyway. What can you do about it? The law's on my side.'

This rang equally untrue; probably in contrast, Maigret had never given such an impression of calm and confident authority.

He was huge. When he went under the electric-light bulb he touched it with his head, and his shoulders were so wide they filled the whole window space just as the medieval barons, with their puffed out sleeves, fill the frames of old paintings.

He went on tidying up the room, but more slowly now.

'After all, you know very well that I didn't kill him, don't you?' said Saint-Hilaire nervously.

He took his handkerchief from his pocket and blew into it noisily.

'Sit down,' Maigret said to him.

' I prefer to stand. . . .'

'Sit down.'

He obeyed like a frightened child, as soon as the Chief Inspector turned round to him.

He was looking shifty, with the agitated look of a man who feels he is not up to the part he has to play but is still trying to swim against the tide.

'I suppose,' grunted Maigret, 'it won't be necessary to send for the Nevers tax inspector to recognize his old friend Émile Gallet?

'I'd have got at the truth without him. It would have taken longer, that's all. . . .

'I've felt for some time that there was something in this

story which didn't fit. No need for you to try and understand. When all the material evidence combines to confuse things instead of simplifying them, then someone has been laying a false trail.

'And everything, without exception, was false in this case. ... Nothing fitted. ... The shot and the knifing ... The room over the yard and the wall ... The bruise on the left wrist and the lost key ...

'And even the three possible suspects!

'But above all it was Émile Gallet who didn't fit, dead or alive! If the tax inspector hadn't said anything, I would have gone further back into the dead man's past. ... I would have gone right to the *lycée* where I would have got the truth. ... Actually, you can't have stayed long at the *lycée* in Nantes. ...'

'Two years. I was expelled!'

'Of course! You were playing football even then! And most probably running after the girls! You see how it doesn't fit? Look at this photograph! No, look at it! When you were jumping over the wall of the *lycée* to meet your girl friends, this poor fellow was having to take care of his liver.

'It would have taken me some time to collect all the proof. ... It made no difference that I knew the main point. ... This man, who suddenly needed twenty thousand francs, was in Sancerre for the sole purpose of asking you for them. ...

'And you saw him *twice*! And in the evening you saw him on top of the wall! You were sure he was going to kill himself, weren't you? Perhaps he even told you as much?'

'No. But he did seem wrought up. In the afternoon, I was struck by the jerky way he spoke.'

'You refused him his twenty thousand francs?'

'I couldn't do anything else, because it would have happened again and again. ... In the end I am quite sure I would have been down to my last penny. ...'

'Was it when working for your notary in Saigon, that you heard he was heir to a fortune?'

'Yes, an odd-looking client came to see my boss. An old

crank, who had lived in the bush for more than twenty years and who hadn't seen a white man for three. He was eaten up with fever and opium smoking. . . . I was there during the conversation. . . . "I'll be gone pretty soon," he said, "and I don't even know if there's anyone of my family left anywhere. . . . Perhaps there is a Saint-Hilaire, but I doubt it, because when I left France the last one left was so seedy-looking that he must have died of consumption. If there is an heir and you can get hold of him, then he will be my sole legatee."

'So, even then you had thought about getting rich quick!' said Maigret dreamily.

And, looking beyond the man before him, fifty years old, sweating and embarrassed, he felt he could see the gay, strapping unscrupulous fellow who had organized a ludicrous ceremony in order to get himself a native girl.

'Carry on.'

'I should have had to return to France, anyway, because of women. . . . I had gone a bit too far there. . . . There were husbands, brothers, and fathers who were after me. . . .

'I got the idea of looking for a Saint-Hilaire and that was not easy. . . . I got track of Tiburce through the *lycée* in Bourges. They told me they didn't know what had become of him. But I got from them the fact that he was a gloomy, reserved young man, who had never had a friend at school. . . .'

'Good Lord, of course he hadn't!' laughed Maigret. 'He hadn't a penny to his name. Nothing but his board paid for until he had finished his education.'

'My idea, at the time, was to split the inheritance, by some means or other, I didn't know how. . . . But I then realized it would be more difficult to split it than to take it all. . . .

'It took me three months to find him – at Le Havre, where he was trying to get taken on as a steward or interpreter aboard a passenger-liner. . . .

'He had ten or twelve francs left in his pocket; I offered him a drink, then I had to drag all his background out of him bit by bit. . . . Even then he only answered in monosyllables.

'He had been a private tutor in a château, proof-reader for a publisher in Rouen, clerk in a book shop.

'He was wearing a ridiculous morning-coat and he had a silly, scraggy beard, reddish-brown. . . .

'I played for high stakes. I told him how I wanted to make my fortune in America, and that nothing helped a man more over there than a title to one's name, especially with the women. . . .

'I suggested to him that I buy his name. I had a little money, since my father, who was a horse dealer in Nantes, had left me a bit.

'I paid him thirty thousand francs for the right to call myself Tiburce de Saint-Hilaire. . . .'

Maigret shot a brief glance at the picture, looked the other up and down, and finally stared so fixedly at him that he began again without further prompting and with unnatural emphasis.

'A business man does the same when he buys shares at two hundred francs knowing he will be able to sell at five times that price a month later, doesn't he? I had to wait years for the legacy. The old idiot down in the jungle refused to die. . . . And *I* was the one without money who starved. . . .

'We were almost the same age. . . . All we had to do was to exchange papers. He had simply to undertake never to set foot in Nantes, where he might have met someone who knew me.

'As far as I was concerned hardly any precautions were necessary. The real Tiburce had never had any friends. . . . More often than not, when he took a job, he wouldn't give his real name as he was rather embarrassed about it. . . . Who's ever heard of a clerk in a book shop called Tiburce de Saint-Hilaire?

'At last! I read a little notice in the papers announcing the legacy, and asking the beneficiaries, if there were any, to come forward.

'So now do you think I didn't earn the one million, two hundred thousand francs the old bush-man left?'

Encouraged by Maigret's silence he had recovered his self-assurance, and for two pins he would have given him a wink.

'Of course, in the meantime Gallet had got married, and wasn't exactly rolling in money; as soon as he heard, he came running along and cursed me so savagely that for a moment I thought he was going to kill me. . . .

'I offered him ten thousand francs, which he finally decided to take. . . . But he came back six months later. . . . And again after that . . . He threatened to reveal the truth. I tried to point out to him that he would be convicted just the same as me. . . .

'Besides, there was his family, and he seemed frightened of them. . . .

'Gradually, he calmed down. . . . He had aged very quickly . . . with his morning-coat, pointed beard, yellow skin, and dark-ringed eyes, I felt sorry for him. . . .

'He began to play the beggar. . . . He would always begin by asking for fifty thousand francs. . . . "Once and for all," he would promise! Then, he would go off with one or two thousand-franc notes. . . .

'But if you add up all I've given him over eighteen years! I repeat, if I hadn't been firm, I would have ended up by losing it all.

'I was working too. I looked for good investments, and I put down all the land you can see above the estate to vines . . . What did he do all this time? He made out that he was travelling as representative for a firm, whereas, in fact, the only profession he was following was that of cadging on other people. . . .

'He began to like it. . . . Calling himself Monsieur Clément, as you already know, he would go round hunting people out. . . . Well, you tell me what I should have done.'

His voice rose. Without thinking he got up.

'On the Saturday in question, he wanted twenty thousand francs immediately. Even if I had felt like giving it to him, I wouldn't have been able to as the banks were closed. . . . And, anyway, hadn't I paid enough?

'I told him so; I called him a good-for-nothing. . . . He tried again that afternoon putting on such a humble act I was nearly sick. A man has no right to let himself go down to that extent. . . . Life is a gamble . . . you win or lose! But even so you keep a bit of self-respect. . . .'

'You told him that as well?' interrupted Maigret, surprisingly gently.

'Why shouldn't I? I wanted to brace him up a bit. . . . I suggested five hundred francs.'

Leaning on the mantelpiece, the Chief Inspector drew the portrait of the dead man towards him.

'Five hundred francs,' he repeated.

'I'll show you the book where I note all my expenses down, and it will prove to you that, in all, he has squeezed two hundred thousand francs out of me. . . . That evening, I was in the park . . .'

'Not altogether happy . . .'

'I was nervous, I don't know why; I heard a noise by the wall. Then I saw him doing something or other up in the tree. . . . I couldn't see what. At first, I thought he wanted to do me in. . . .

'But he disappeared as quickly as he came. . . . I climbed on to a barrel. . . . He had gone back to his room, and was standing up near the table, facing me. . . . He could not see me. . . . I didn't understand. . . . I promise you, that at that moment I was frightened. The shot rang out ten yards away from me and Gallet didn't move. Only his right cheek went all red. . . . Blood was flowing. . . . He went on standing quite still, his eyes fixed all the time on the same spot as if he were waiting for something. . . .'

Maigret took the revolver off the mantelpiece. A length of metal-bound gut, of the kind used for pike fishing, was still tied to it.

Under the barrel was fixed a little tin box, connected to the trigger by a stiff wire.

Maigret flicked open the box with a finger-nail, revealing a little machine exactly like those on general sale for taking self-portraits. It consisted merely of a spring which when wound up released itself a few seconds later.

However, in this case it was a triple action device and consequently should have produced three explosions.

'The spring must have jammed after the first shot,' he said in a slow rather muffled tone.

The last words his companion had spoken rang in his ears!

'Only his right cheek was all red. . . . Blood was flowing. He went on standing quite still, his eyes fixed all the time on the same spot, as if he were waiting for something. . . .'

Of course! The other two bullets – he had not been sure how accurate it would be. With three bullets he was sure of getting at least one in the head! And the other two had not gone off! He had taken his knife from his pocket.

'He staggered after he had thrust the knife into his chest. . . . He fell like a stone where he was. . . . He was dead, of course, and my first thought was that it was revenge and that he would have made sure to leave papers behind, which would reveal the truth, and perhaps even accuse me of killing him. . . .'

'You are a cautious man; and you have presence of mind; so you went off to look for rubber gloves in the kitchen.'

'Would I go and leave my finger-prints in the room, now? I went through the gate. . . . I put the key in my pocket. . . . My visit was of no avail. . . . He had burnt all his papers himself . . . I was afraid. . . . His eyes were open and they upset me. . . I went back in such a hurry I forgot to lock the gate. . . . What would you have done in my shoes, seeing that he was well and truly dead?

'I was even more afraid that evening when I was playing cards at the notary's and heard that the gun had fired again. . . I went to take a close look at it. . . . I did not dare to touch it, because if they started suspecting me that gun would be the main factor in proving my innocence.

'It's an automatic six-shooter; I realized that the spring had jammed on the first shot, and had freed itself a week later owing to some change in the atmospheric conditions.

'But three more bullets could still be there, couldn't they? From that moment I spent my time hanging around in the park listening . . . Just now, for instance, while we were both in this room, I took care not to stand near the table. . . .'

'But you didn't stop me! It was you who threw the key into the road when I threatened to search your house. . . .'

The hotel visitors, their dinner over, were taking their evening walk, and their footsteps could be heard on the road. From the kitchen came the intermittent clatter of plates being stacked.

'I was wrong to offer you money. . . .'

Maigret nearly burst out laughing, and if he had not managed to suppress it, it would probably have been a rather frightening laugh.

Standing in front of his companion, who was a head shorter than he was, and with shoulders only half as wide, he looked at him with a mixture of hatred and pity, his hand poised as though to seize him suddenly by the scruff of the neck or smash his head against the wall.

And yet there was something pitiful about the fake Tiburce de Saint-Hilaire's desire to justify himself, to recapture his self-confidence.

A miserable little rascal who hadn't the courage to admit his rascality, who probably didn't altogether realize what a rascal he was.

And here he was trying to brazen it out! He drew back rapidly whenever Maigret showed signs of moving; if the Chief Inspector had raised his arm, he would almost certainly have taken cover on the floor.

'Of course, if his wife needs anything I am ready to help her, on the quiet, and as far as my means allow. . . .'

He knew that the law was on his side, but even so! He wasn't happy about it; he would have given a lot for a good word from the detective, who seemed to be playing cat-and-mouse with him.

'He has made provision for her himself. . . .'

'Yes, I read that in the papers. An insurance worth three hundred thousand francs! . . . It's fantastic! . . .'

Maigret could contain himself no longer:

'Fantastic, isn't it? This man who spent his childhood without having a single farthing for pocket money! You know the *lycées*. . . .

'Most of the big families of central France send their sons to Bourges. . . . Saint-Hilaire is a fine name, a name as old and splendid as the rest of them; there was only this ridiculous Christian name of Tiburce.

'Now what about him – he goes to the regular meals and attends the classes but he hasn't the wherewithal to buy a bar of chocolate, a whistle, or even some marbles. . . . During recreation periods, he is always alone in a corner. . . . Perhaps the junior staff, who are almost as poor as he is, take pity on him. . . .

'He leaves the place and sells old books in a shop. He trails hopelessly from one job to another, with his portmanteau of a name, his morning-coat, and his liver trouble.

'He has nothing he can pawn, but he has this name, which, one fine day, somebody offers to buy from him.

'It's still a miserable existence, but at least he's got rid of the name. With the name of Gallet, he is one up – he is ordinary. . . . And he's got enough to keep body and soul together. . .

'Only his new family treat him like an outcast.

'He has a wife and son. . . . And his wife and son upbraid him for his inability to get on, to earn money, or become a County Councillor like his brother-in-law. . . .

'And now the name which he has sold for three hundred thousand francs is suddenly worth more than a million. The only thing he ever possessed; the very thing which had brought him the most misery and humiliation; the thing he had shaken off!

'And the former Gallet, a gay dog, a strapping fellow, hands him out a little charity from time to time.

'Fantastic, you say! Nothing succeeded with him. He was eating his heart out all his life! No one even gave him a helping hand.

'His son kicked over the traces and left as soon as he could to make his own way in life leaving the old man to go on being ordinary.

'Only his wife was resigned to it; I wouldn't say she was any comfort to him or that she helped him. *She was resigned*, because she felt there was nothing that could be done. He was just a pathetic man on a diet!

'And he left her three hundred thousand francs! More than she had ever had during his lifetime. Three hundred thousand francs – enough to send her sister running to her and to get a smile of approval from the County Councillor.

'For five years he carries on. He has one liver attack after another. The Legitimists give no more than they would to a beggar. He wheedles a thousand-franc note out of them, now and then.

'But a Monsieur Jacob takes from him the best part of what he has managed to scrounge in this way.

'Extraordinary, isn't it – Gallet–Saint-Hilaire! Even though he has to cut down his own meagre expenses, he keeps up this life-insurance, paying more than twenty thousand francs a year.

'He knows that the time is coming when despair will get the better of him, unless his heart gives up of its own . . .

'A poor man, all alone, coming and going, never at home anywhere, except perhaps when he goes fishing and is all alone.

'He was born under an evil star, his family was going downhill and, what's more, they made the cardinal error of devoting the few thousand francs they had managed to save to his schooling. He made a bad deal over the sale of his name. He made a bad deal working on the royalist net just when the cause was at its last gasp.

'He made a bad deal over his marriage; his son takes after his sisters and brothers-in-law!

'People die every day, when they don't want to, when they are happy and in good health; but he couldn't die, even though he wanted to. And the insurance company won't pay in a case of suicide!

'He plays about with watches and springs.... He knows only too well that the moment is not far off when he will be able to go no further.

'Finally, Monsieur Jacob demands twenty thousand francs! He hasn't got it! Nobody will give it to him! He has the spring in his pocket. To appease his conscience, he knocks at the door of the man who got a million instead of him....

'He has no hope.... And yet he comes back. But already he has asked for a room overlooking the yard, because he is not sure of the machine and prefers the more simple procedure with the well....

'He has led a distorted, luckless life.

'What happens? The room over the yard is not free. So now he has to climb the wall after all!

'And two bullets don't go off! You yourself said: "*His cheek was all red.... Blood was flowing.... He remained standing quite still, his eyes fixed all the time on the same spot as though he were waiting for something....*" Did he not spend his whole life waiting for something? A *little* bit of luck . . . Not even that! One of those lucky breaks, which happen so often and most people don't even notice.

'And he even had to wait for his last two bullets, which never came.

'He has to finish the job himself.'

Maigret stopped and suddenly clenched his jaw so hard that the stem of his pipe broke clean in two between his teeth. And his companion, looking away, finding it difficult to speak, muttered:

'Doesn't alter the fact that he was a swindler!'

Maigret looked at him for a full minute, without a motion,

his eyes blazing. His great hand was raised; he felt the owner of the 'little château' tense with fear; he kept his hand in mid-air as though enjoying this moment of panic and, finally, tapped the man on the shoulder:

'You are right! He was a swindler! As for you, the law's on your side, isn't it?'

'You should know the law better than I do, but I should think ...'

'But, of course! Of course! There's the legal right! And the law lays down that no offence or crime has been committed if a son gets hold of his father's possessions by fraud ... which means that like you Henri Gallet has nothing to fear. Up to now, he has only collected a hundred thousand francs ... Which with his mistress's fifty thousand only makes one hundred and fifty thousand, and he needs five hundred thousand to go and live in the country, as the doctors say he should. You said it, Monsieur de Saint-Hilaire! Fantastic! There is no crime! There is no murderer – no one is guilty! No one to put in prison.

'Or, rather, there would have been only my poor dead friend, if he hadn't had the sound idea of putting himself out of reach of justice; in the cemetery at Saint-Fargeau under a *headstone not too expensive, but in good taste and distinguished.*

'Give me a light! Oh – don't worry about your left hand *now*....

'Moreover, there is no reason why you should deny yourself the pleasure of starting up a football club in Sancerre now. You can be the Patron....'

Abruptly, his face changed, and he said:

'Get out ...'

'But ... I ...'

'Get out!'

Once more Saint-Hilaire wavered, and it was several seconds before he regained his composure.

'I think you're exaggerating, Inspector.... If ...'

'Not by the door ... Through the window! You know the way, don't you? Wait! You've forgotten your key....'

'When you have calmed down a bit, I'll . . .'

'That's it! You'll send me a crate of that sparkling wine you once offered me. . . .'

Saint-Hilaire didn't know whether he ought to smile or be frightened. He saw Maigret's great bulk advancing toward him and instinctively he retreated to the window.

'You haven't given me your address . . .'

'I'll send it to you on a post-card . . . Hop it! Remember, you are still agile for your age!'

He closed the window with a bang and found himself once more alone in the bedroom now staring in the hard light of the single electric bulb.

The bed was just as Émile Gallet must have found it when he came into the room; the black morning-coat of hard-wearing cloth was hanging all limp from the wall. Maigret snatched the portrait irritably off the mantelpiece, slipped it into a buff envelope with the Criminal Records office heading, and wrote Madame Gallet's address on it.

It was shortly after ten. The click of heels could be heard from the terrace where people who had come out from Paris by car were dancing to a portable gramophone.

They were trying to dance, while Monsieur Tardivon, torn between his respect for the flashy car and the protestations of the inmates of the hotel who had already gone to bed, tried to talk them into going into one of the rooms inside.

Maigret walked down the corridor, through the café where a carrier was playing billiards with the schoolmaster, and arrived outside, where he found a couple fox-trotting. They stopped suddenly.

'What did he say?'

'He said the people staying in the hotel were already in bed. . . . He wants us to make less noise.'

The two lights on the suspension bridge were visible, and, now and then, they were reflected in the river Loire.

'Can't we dance?'

'Only inside . . .'

'Oh! It would have been so romantic!'

Monsieur Tardivon, looking very formal, was conducting this argument, while looking longingly at the car owned by these difficult people; he suddenly noticed Maigret.

'I have had your place laid in the morning-room, Inspector. Well – any news?'

The gramophone went on playing. On the first floor a woman in a frilly bodice was watching the intruders and calling to her husband, who must have been in bed:

'Go down and tell them to shut up! It's a bit much, if you can't even go to sleep any more!'

On the other side, another couple – probably a shop assistant and a typist – were on the side of the motorists in the hope of striking up an acquaintance and thereby spending a less boring evening than usual.

'I'm not going to have any dinner,' Maigret announced. 'Would you please get my things taken to the station?'

'For the eleven thirty-two? Are you going, then?'

'I am off.'

'All the same . . . Surely you'll have something to eat. . . . At least, take one of the hotel cards.'

Monsieur Tardivon took a picture post-card out of his pocket; to judge by the poor quality of the reproduction and the women's fashions, it must have been at least twelve years old.

The picture showed the Hôtel de la Loire with the terrace crowded with people and a flag flying from the first floor. Monsieur Tardivon was there in evening-dress, standing smiling at the front entrance, and the waitresses, plates in hand, were posed in front of the camera.

'Thank you . . .'

Maigret stuffed the card into one of his pockets, and turned for one second to look up Nettle Lane.

In the 'little château' a light suddenly appeared in a window and Maigret was sure that Tiburce de Saint-Hilaire was there, about to undress, muttering to himself: 'He had to listen to reason in the end, after all! . . . First of all, I have a legal right to it. . . . I know my Roman Law just as well as he does. . . . And he knows it! Besides, Gallet was nothing but a crook. . . . Yes . . . And nobody can blame *me* for anything, now, can they?'

But perhaps he was looking somewhat fearfully into the dark corners of the room?

At Saint-Fargeau, the light in Madame Gallet's bedroom would be out. She would be patting the empty place beside her, her hair in curlers, temporarily relieved of the burden of her dignity; and perhaps before getting off to sleep she would sob quietly under the bed-clothes.

But of course she had her sister to console her and the County Councillor – her brother-in-law. Soon they would have her back in the comfortable atmosphere of the family circle.

Maigret shook hands limply with a somewhat distrait Monsieur Tardivon, watching the motorists, who had now decided to dine and dance inside.

His footsteps echoed on the deserted suspension bridge. There was a barely audible murmur of water swirling round the sandbanks.

Then he comforted himself with the thought of Henry, in similar surroundings, older, his complexion more sallow, his mouth wider and thinner, with an Éléonore whose features would have hardened with age and whose figure would gradually have grown less attractive. They would be quarrelling. Over everything, and over nothing! Mostly over *their* five hundred thousand francs! . . . They would be bound to get that much! . . . 'How can you talk like that . . . your father was a . . .' 'I forbid you to speak about my father. . . . What about you, anyway: when I first met you . . .?' 'You knew very well what I was . . .'

*

He slept right through to Paris; a heavy sleep, peopled with indistinct figures, all swarming about in a sickening fashion.

In the buffet of the Gare de Lyon he gulped down some

coffee with a dash of alcohol. When he came to pay he inadvertently drew out of his pocket the picture post-card of the Hôtel de la Loire. Beside him a shop girl was eating a croissant which she dipped into her bowl of chocolate.

He left the card on the counter. When he turned round again outside, he saw the girl looking dreamily at the trees surrounding Monsieur Tardivon's hotel and the end of the suspension bridge.

Perhaps she will sleep in that room, he mused. And Saint-Hilaire would invite her to drink a glass of sparkling wine with him on his estate!

'You look as though you have just come from a funeral!' remarked Madame Maigret, when he got home to his flat in Boulevard Richard-Lenoir. . . . 'Have you had something to eat?'

'I have . . .' he said to himself, looking round, happy to be back in the familiar surroundings. 'From the moment he was buried . . .'

He added, though she couldn't have understood, 'However, I would rather deal with a real genuine corpse, killed by a proper murderer. . . . Will you wake me at eleven o'clock? . . . I have to go and make my report to the boss. . . .'

He did not admit that he had no intention of sleeping, but that instead he was puzzling over what sort of a report he would write.

Was he to tell the truth, pure and simple, which would not only rob Madame Gallet of three hundred thousand francs insurance, but would also set her against her son, against Éléonore, and against Tiburce de Saint-Hilaire, and once more against her sisters and brothers-in-law?

That would produce a tangle of conflicting interests, mutual hatreds, and never-ending law-suits. . . . It was even possible that some painstaking judge would have Émile Gallet exhumed for re-examination!

Maigret no longer had the photograph of the dead man, but there was no need now of that faded likeness.

'His cheek was all red. . . . Blood was flowing. . . . He went on standing quite still, his eyes fixed on the same spot, as though he were waiting for something.'

'Peace, of course! That's what he was waiting for!' roared Maigret, getting up well before the time he had said.

And, a little later, shoulders hunched, he was saying to his chief: 'A wash-out! Nothing to do but file this nasty little case away.'

Meanwhile he was working it out:

'According to the doctor, he would not have lived more than three years. So let's say the insurance company has lost sixty-thousand francs. . . . But, after all, its capital is ninety million.'

MORE ABOUT PENGUINS AND PELICANS

MAIGRET AND THE ENIGMATIC LETT

Pietr-le-Letton was among the very earliest Simenons. It must be the most tortuous puzzle of identities ever handled by Maigret.

Pietr the Lett had for years been clocked across the frontiers by Interpol: he had the personality of a chameleon. Apart from his extraordinary resemblance to the twisted corpse they found in the toilet of the Pole Star express when she drew into the Gare du Nord, he passed as Mr Oswald Oppenheim, immaculate friend of the Mortimer-Levingstons, multi-millionaires; he seemed to be Olaf Swaan, the Norwegian merchant officer of Fécamp; and he was Fédor Yurovich, a down-and-out Russian drunk from the Paris ghetto, to the life. Maigret needed the obstinate nose of a basset-hound to run down this dangerous international crook. He nearly lost his life once and, when they killed his old friend Inspector Torrence, nearly lost his head as well. But he was in at the kill.

MAIGRET'S FIRST CASE

Here is a new Maigret indeed – young, recently wedded, and fresh to his job. It was always known that he started as secretary to the superintendent in a local Paris police station. In this book Simenon, with his usual mastery of period and setting, tells how Maigret got his first chance, and allows us some touching glimpses of the newly-wed Madame Maigret. In the social pattern of 1913 it was no easy task for a young country-bred policeman to penetrate the secrets of a wealthy and influential family. But trust Maigret to find friends in the local *brasserie*: this time it was the little flautist in the band who helped him in his inquiries. After a narrow shave at the hands of two deceptively jolly toughs, Maigret was in a position to unmask the crooks when he was checked from a totally unexpected direction.

Not for sale in the U.S.A. or Canada

MAIGRET MEETS A MILORD

This famous Maigret, first published as *Le Charretier de la 'Providence'*, marks Simenon's entry into the damp world of barges and towpath-cafés which is one of his special provinces. It is also the case in which Maigret extracted, by signs, a confession from a dying man.

Jean the carter – half man, half bear – possessed vital evidence about the death of Mary Lampson, found strangled in a stable near Lock 14 at Dizy in Champagne. Her husband, Sir William Lampson, a retired colonel, was unconcerned, curt, and arrogant when Maigret questioned him on board his yacht. A rare old whisky-logged life they seem to have led, too, along the inland waterways – with Lampson's mistress, his wife's paramour, and light little ladies from Montparnasse. But how to pin the blame? When Maigret took to a bicycle he was able to draw together the strands of a strange and pitiful story.

MAIGRET AT THE CROSSROADS

Translated from *La Nuit du carrefour*, this is the story of Maigret's classic vigil at the crossroads. An unforgettable night, vibrating like a concert grand with action and tension.

Twenty miles south of Paris they found the corpse of a Jewish diamond-merchant from Antwerp. Nobody knew him. The body was in M. Michonnet's car. But M. Michonnet's car was in Carl Andersen's garage. And Carl Andersen, a Dane, hadn't budged under seventeen hours of interrogation. He had heard nothing: his languid sister had been locked into her bedroom all night. Michonnet was the pompous soul of respectability injured, and at the third house by the crossroads the traffic simply came and went, in search of petrol, at the garage of the vulgar Monsieur Oscar. Nobody knew a thing.

Then the diamond-merchant's widow was shot down in the dark at Maigret's feet, and the chief inspector plunged into action like a wounded buffalo, as ponderous, as merciless, and as cunning.

MAIGRET AND THE HUNDRED GIBBETS

First published as *Le Pendu de St Pholien*, this early Simenon records how Maigret unwittingly drove a little man to suicide.

You'd have said that Louis Jeunet was a down-at-heel layabout, but he was packeting up over 30,000 francs when Maigret first spotted him in Brussels. When he posted the money, unregistered, as 'Printed Matter', Maigret followed him for fun. He took a train for the north. At the German frontier Maigret switched suitcases, in a spirit of idle curiosity, but when Jeunet discovered his loss at Bremen he took out a gun and shot himself, and Maigret was left to cope with his own culpability. His subsequent inquiries provoked two attempts on his life and eventually led to Liège, Simenon's birthplace, where in a crazy slum he taps the source of a macabre story which is reminiscent of François Villon.

MAIGRET MYSTIFIED

In this early Maigret, published in 1932 as *L'Ombre chinoise*, Simenon sketches a genteel underworld of old jealousies, stifled hatreds, and concealed relationships.

A few facts were clear. M. Couchet had been shot dead in an armchair in the office of his pharmaceutical firm, adjoining a block of flats in the quiet Place des Vosges. It was nearing midnight. And three hundred thousand francs were missing. Since the chair was still jammed against the safe, theft must have preceded murder.

But, in that case, why had Couchet taken a seat face to face with the thief? (Or had there been two unrelated crimes?) Maigret found himself more and more mystified by the eerie shadow-show of life in this block of flats, where dim shapes moved across the dark courtyard, women watched at windows or listened at doors, and tenants scrabbled in the dustbins.